Family Past

Ellie McLellan Genealogy Mystery - Book 10

Beth Farrar

Edited by Ronnie Pelletier

Cover by GetCovers.com

First edition published – 2025

eBook ISBN: **978-1-997869-00-9**

Paperback ISBN: 978-1-997869-01-6

Hardcover ISBN: 978-1-997869-02-3

Large Print ISBN: 978-1-997860-03-0

Author's Note: Being a Canadian author, please excuse any double "l"s or wayward "u"s in words, eh. Please do not flag them. Much appreciated.

Also by

Ellie McLellan Genealogy Mystery Series

Family Secrets – Book 1
Family Mistakes – Book 2
Family Promises – Book 3
Family Crimes – Book 4
Family Christmas – Book 5
Family Links – Book 6
Family Ties – Book 7
Family Vows – Book 8
Family Loss – Book 9
Family Gathering – Novella

Sign up for my newsletter at bethfarrar.com!

Receive a free PDF with tons of ideas on how to write your own memoir, find out what I'm working on next!

You never know what you'll find.

This book is dedicated to my ancestors. The ones who overcame tragedy to start anew, who fought wars, and travelled oceans to begin new lives. And to those who had blessedly normal lives but showed me how a calm and gentle life is one of the most underrated gifts one can have.

Contents

Chapter One

"France?" Ellie's eyes flew open wide, all remaining thoughts of snuggling back under the covers with her husband that cool autumn morning now tossed aside. She jumped out of bed and glanced around frantically. "How long do I have to pack?" She dashed into the cupboard and dragged out a suitcase almost half her five-foot size and plopped it in the middle of the room.

"Slow down," Quinn mumbled, brushing his hair out of his eyes and squinting at her. He was usually an early riser, most often out in the barn working on his furniture commissions before Ellie had even cracked open an eye. "We're not leaving until tonight." He threw his head back against his pillow and groaned. They had spent the previous night at a Montreal restaurant and had stopped on Mount Royal to watch the full moon before arriving home late. "Maggie was right. I should have given you more time."

Ellie froze, her dresser drawer open and a handful of socks waving in the air. "You mean Maggie knew where we were going all this time?"

Quinn sat up and swung out of bed. Unbunching his t-shirt from around his chest, he stretched his arms in the air. Ellie was momentarily thrown off topic by the sight of her husband.

"I *had* to tell your best friend," Quinn told her. "She had some helpful suggestions on how to handle the whole trip."

"Oh, I bet she did." Ellie snorted. She threw the socks back in the drawer and slammed it shut with a bang.

Quinn grimaced. He reached for her hand and drew her back to sit on the bed beside him. Wrapping his arm around her shoulders he waited until he felt she was calm enough to actually hear what he said.

"Are we going to Paris?" Ellie whispered, a grin replacing the frown. "Can we go up the Eiffel Tower?"

He gathered her close and kissed the top of her head. "Your fear of heights might cause a problem with that, but we can do anything you want to do. I've booked a hotel for a few days in Paris and then..."

Ellie jumped up and faced him, her hands waving excitedly. "Can we go on a road trip?"

He raised an eyebrow, knowing full well where she was headed. "I think we can manage that. Any place in particular?" He watched her jitter from side to side, as if an electric current was coursing through her.

"You know full well my Ethier family comes from Rivièreclaire." She stopped and frowned. "I wonder how far it is from Paris."

"It's approximately four hundred and nineteen kilometres," Quinn said. "We could take a train to Limoges then hire a taxi."

Ellie dove at him, driving him backwards onto the bed. She took his face in her hands and kissed him deeply. "You knew all along, didn't you? That I wanted to go there?"

He rolled her off him and onto her side, turning to face her and running his finger down her cheek. "I wasn't sure you'd want to get on a plane again, but you handled the visit to Scotland like a pro. I thought this trip would be something to remember."

Ellie slapped her forehead dramatically. "I forgot! I have to fly there."

"We could do something else, if you want," Quinn said, not sure if she was joking. "But I've already made the reservations."

She poked him in the chest and laughed. "Not a chance. This is going to be the best honeymoon anyone ever had." She threw her arms around his neck and held on tight. The quiet settled on them and she pulled back slowly. "I mean it. This is the best thing you could have given me. I love you." She leaned in for a kiss just as their golden retriever, Cali, came bounding into the room, onto the bed, and stuck her head between them.

"Down you furry beast." Ellie pushed the dog away as Cali gave her a wet sloppy good morning lick.

Quinn stood and pulled Ellie up beside him. "My plan is—Ruth, Shirley, and Jeremy will stay here and look after the pup for us." Ellie leaned into him for a quick hug, her head reaching his collarbone.

"And Samantha will take Cali out for walks and play?" Ellie asked.

"Already arranged." Quinn's smile was smug.

"So, everything at the homestead is settled. I guess everyone else knew when we were leaving too?"

"You look like a delighted little elf right now." He grinned back at her. "*My* little elf."

"This is true."

"You're not the only one who likes to dot their I's and cross their T's." He winked at her and headed for the bathroom. He stopped at the door and turned. "You've got hours to pack. Maggie thought you'd like to take some family records as well."

Ellie clapped her hands. "I can't believe I'm going to finally see where my ancestors came from." She spun around, glancing at her suitcase, her laptop, and then settling on Cali who had planted herself at Ellie's feet and was patiently waiting. "But first you and I will take a long walk, Cali."

"You can make your list on your phone as you walk," Quinn called out over his shoulder before he disappeared into the bathroom.

Ellie scrambled into a pair of jeans and threw on a t-shirt and sweater before bounding down the stairs to the main floor, Cali at her heels. Ellie grabbed her phone from the table, shoved her feet into her running shoes and dashed out the door towards the woods.

She had so much to plan.

***

Ellie opened the door to the Cozy Corner Café half an hour later. The tinkling of the bell had heads turning her way as she hurried in. Cali watched her through the glass door from where Ellie had tied her leash to a wooden bench. The dog's head tilted one way and then another, as if wondering why she couldn't follow her human inside.

"Look at that poor darling," Maggie crooned as she came around the main counter and gave her best friend a hug.

"I'm not a poor darling," Ellie scoffed.

Maggie laughed. "I meant Cali." She disappeared into the kitchen and returned with a bowl full of water and a dog biscuit.

"Oops. With all the excitement, I totally forgot to feed her this morning."

Maggie shook her head. She marched out the door, placed the water bowl in the shade, and gave Cali her treat. A few rubs later, Maggie was back inside and washing her hands. She pulled a carrot muffin from the display case and poured Ellie a cup of coffee. "Let's sit a bit." She led Ellie to a small table in the corner. "I've got a few minutes before the hordes arrive."

"So business is good?" Ellie asked, taking in the full shelves of Maggie's pastries and baked goods awaiting the morning customers.

Maggie motioned to the car park, where three cars had just turned in. "Better every day. Fall used to be slow, but since Sara put hiking paths in the woods behind the Tiny House Haven Community, people come up to spend time in nature."

"She's done an amazing job turning the Haven into a growing business," Ellie said before taking a huge bite of her muffin.

"Slow down," Maggie said. "You'll get indigestion. Have you packed yet?"

The twinkle in her eye, and obvious excitement for her friend, had Ellie's shoulders lower from around her ears. She let out a deep breath and sank back in her seat. "I can't believe he's taking me to France," Ellie said, failing miserably at keeping the grin off her face.

"Your husband is very thoughtful."

"He is that." Ellie sipped her coffee. "He's also taking me to my ancestor's hometown." Her leg started jiggling up and down.

Maggie reached over and put her hand on Ellie's knee. "You've got all day to pack. Your ancestor information can be accessed on your phone through Ancestry. You've got way too much time on your hands right now. You need to settle down a bit."

"But I need more time to..." Ellie started but stopped when Maggie's grandfather, Graham Brody, and Ellie's Aunt Norma walked into the Café. They were sharing a laugh and Norma gave Graham a friendly nudge in the arm.

Maggie and Ellie gave each other a look. Ellie leaned towards her friend. "What's going on with those two?"

"Norma's helping him move his last few things from upstairs." Maggie headed back to the counter to serve them. "What can I get you two boomers today?"

Ellie gasped, but Norma and Graham laughed even harder. "It's a compliment," Graham assured Ellie.

"Oh, Maggie," Norma said as she caught her breath. "You are the cat's meow!"

Maggie sent Ellie a sideways glance. "Thank you, I think."

Graham walked around the counter and gave her a hug. "We don't mind being reminded how old we are. We're lucky to be healthy and alive."

"We work hard at it," Norma reminded them. She hurried to Ellie and hugged her. "Are you okay? You look like you're running a fever." She put the back of her hand to Ellie's forehead and frowned. "Nope."

"Quinn is taking her to Paris for their honeymoon," Maggie said, shifting two mugs onto a tray and filling them with coffee. "They fly out tonight," she added, placing honey muffins on plates on the tray before handing it off to her grandfather. "Want me to carry this for you?"

"I'm old; I'm not broken," Graham scoffed, the twinkle in his eyes taking the sting from his declaration. "Paris, eh? Well, isn't that something?" He said, balancing the tray and pacing carefully across the café to Norma with Maggie following. "I remember Paris during the war. I was only passing through then, but it's a beautiful city." He and Norma settled at a table next to Ellie and Maggie's.

"Isn't our family from France?" Norma asked Ellie.

Ellie nodded, the last piece of muffin disappearing into her mouth. Chewing quickly, she said, "And he's taking me to their hometown."

Norma grinned. "Now that's love. Following your better half around while they do something they love to do, even if it bores you to tears."

"Norma!" Graham admonished. "I doubt very much Quinn is bored when he's with Ellie, no matter what they're doing."

Norma frowned. "I'm sure you're right. Sorry for my lack of a filter, Ellie."

"I know what you mean, Aunt Norma." Ellie stood. "No worries. I've got to get back, feed Cali properly, and get my things in order. Will you let the Heritage Harvesters know there won't be a meeting this week, please?"

"Not to worry," Graham said. "I'll pass the word around. Norma has kindly offered to help me settle in and unpack. I'm still shocked by how much I actually brought."

"It'll be like Christmas in the fall," Norma assured him. "Who knows what you'll find."

The door chime tinkled, heralding more customers, and Maggie returned to work. "Just remember," she called out to her grandfather, "you can get rid of anything you don't want to keep."

"Never was a hoarder," Graham said, giving Ellie a hug. "Have a wonderful time, and take lots of pictures."

Norma was next, wrapping her arms around her niece, pulling her close. "You're very brave to get back on a plane. You've got more courage than you know." She stepped back and pulled a small clunky envelope from her sweater pocket and pushed it into Ellie's hand. "When Quinn told me where he was taking you, I... If you have a minute, can you deliver this for me? It's in Paris, near the Opera Garnier."

Ellie blinked and frowned. "Quinn told you, too?"

Norma shrugged.

Ellie looked at the address on the envelope. *Claudette Beaudet.* "Wait. Isn't this the reclusive fashion designer?"

"She's also my pen-pal," Norma said with a wink. "We've been writing since the war. I want to make sure she gets this safely. And give this to her from me as well." She kissed Ellie's cheek, gave her a deep hug, then returned to her seat as if the bombshell revelation of having a celebrity pen-pal for decades was nothing more than a comment about the weather. Norma fixed her attention to her cup, avoiding Ellie's gaze.

Startled by her aunt's request and now intense interest in her coffee, Ellie looked again at the envelope, felt the heft of it, realizing it was more a small package than a mere letter. Snapping out of the fog of a thousand questions she wanted to ask her aunt, she slipped it into her purse and rushed across the café and around the counter.

Maggie gathered her in for a hug and a whispered "Have the best time."

Ellie squeezed her friend. "You know I will." She dashed outside, slipping past more customers coming in—just in time to rescued Cali from an over excited child who wouldn't stop petting Cali's head more firmly than necessary.

"Come along, you furry beast. We're off on an adventure."

Chapter Two

This time, the many noises the plane made taking off and settling into the air, miles above the earth didn't frighten Ellie. At least, not as much. Her fingers were not sunken into Quinn's forearm, and the color returned to her face by the time the "Unfasten Seatbelt" light flashed on.

They were not in premium economy class this time, but did have their three seats to themselves, allowing Quinn more leg room, and Ellie the freedom to sprawl, should she wish. She sat in the middle seat, still not brave enough to gaze out the window, and thankful she wouldn't have to worry about someone crawling over her to get to the washroom.

She could relax. A bit.

"And you had no idea Norma had a pen-pal all these years?" Quinn asked, still focused on the latest bit of information Ellie had shared as they were boarding.

"Not a whisper." Ellie pulled the envelope out of her purse and passed it to him.

"Claudette Beaudet," he read. "And they've been writing since they were kids?" He felt the outline of the USB stick inside.

"Since the end of the war." Ellie pulled her hoodie over her head and sank back in her seat. "I asked her, and all she said was they were matched by a Red Cross project."

"And nothing more?" He handed the envelope back.

"She said she'd fill me in when I got home," Ellie carefully placed it back in her purse and zipped it closed. "Aunt Norma was in a rush. Said she was heading to Graham's to help him unpack a few old boxes of junk."

"Her words?"

Ellie laughed. "Of course. I doubt Graham would have trekked to a new province with boxes only to toss them when he got here."

"Maggie's going to miss having him stay with her," Quinn said. "And him with her."

"It's not every day you find a living grandfather you never knew about," Ellie said. "But they both need their own space. And he's living behind the Cozy Corner Café, so they'll see each other every day."

"He was lucky that tiny house became available," Quinn said.

"Sara's got planning permission to build more," Ellie told him. "And the Tiny House Haven Community is growing. But not *too* fast," she hastened to add.

Quinn stretched his legs and leaned back, his eyes closing. "I'm glad Ruth, Shirley, and Jeremy are at the farm while we're gone."

"Shirley promised not to change anything," Ellie said.

"Do you think it's hard for them to stay in their old childhood home?"

Ellie took a moment before answering. "No. They were ready to move into the smaller house in the community. And I'll never stop Ruth dropping by on her walks. She's even got Jeremy with her sometimes. Shirley just wants to make sure all is well."

"And work on the garden."

"That would be great," Ellie replied with a sigh. "I've never been much of a gardener, though I doubt she's got time with her landscaping business."

"She'll find time," Quinn said, stifling a yawn behind his hand. "And with Samantha walking Cali, they'll all be taken care of."

Ellie eyed him. "Are you going to miss supper? You were up really early today." She risked a quick glance out the window, catching sight of the sun setting behind Mount Royal, St. Joseph's Oratory outlined in the distance.

"Me, miss a meal?" He sat up and comically slapped his cheeks. "Never."

***

"I'd understand if you're too tired to watch Star Wars tonight," Graham said to Norma as they got out of her car at his tiny house. "Especially after helping me all afternoon and cooking me that amazing dinner."

He unlocked his front door and ushered her in before him. A soft light came on as they stepped inside. Norma sighed as she looked around.

"It never fails to amaze me how you can make such a small space so comfortable with a handful of items," she said.

The lounge area held a two-seater couch, a small end table and a blue Persian rug. Ten feet across was the tiny fireplace in the corner beside the hall closet and a small table with two chairs for dining. The built-in bookcases were now filled with Graham's collection, some fiction with brightly colored spines, others drab medical journals, and sketchbooks with mugs of pencil crayons alongside them. A new hobby, he had informed Norma.

A tiny galley kitchen led straight to the bathroom at the back. A set of stairs climbed from the side table in the lounge up to the bedroom loft. The floor at the top of the stairs allowed Graham to stand, as that space had been dropped over the kitchen cabinets area, shifting needed headroom from the first floor to the loft. The bed was high, but no problem for him to get in and out of, and still had plenty of head room for him to sit in bed without smacking his head on the ceiling.

"You know," Norma said, gazing up the staircase. "I wasn't sure a loft would work for you, but I think it's perfect."

"The exercise will do me good," he said, taking her coat and hanging it up.

"By the way, cooking supper was my treat," she said, pulling her CD from her purse and heading straight for his laptop. "I had to drive you home anyway." She wiggled her eyebrows comically.

Graham lifted a box from the couch and looked around, uncertain where exactly to put it.

"That's the last box, right?" Norma asked. She put the CD down. "Let's finish emptying it, and then settle in and relax."

"You're a 'never put off till tomorrow' lady, aren't you?" Graham put the box on the floor in front of the couch and waited as Norma settled in beside him.

"I hate loose ends. You never know what tomorrow will hold, and if you've still got things to do from yesterday, well, that's a bummer."

Graham nodded, and tried to hide a grin. He loved the way Norma talked, the words she used and how open she was about life. He flipped the lid on the box and pulled a handful of beige files from the top.

"What's that?" Norma pointed to the wooden box now visible.

Graham pulled it out and frowned. "This was my father's memory box. To be honest, when he died, I packed it away. I've never opened it."

"Too painful?"

"In a way. We weren't on the best of terms at the end of his life." He sat back on the couch, the box on his lap, his fingers skimming the smooth top. "He died when I was leaving for the war. I thought I knew everything at that age, that I was invincible. I thought he was too." His last words came out in a whisper, as if dredged from the back room of his memory.

Norma gave his arm a squeeze. "I get that. Families can be..."

"Don't get me started on a heap of adjectives." He gave her a soft smile. "Let's see what secrets my dad kept."

"Oh, Graham, that's a horrible thing to say."

"We all have them, Norma. I'm sure you have a few you'll keep till you die."

Norma shrugged, hesitated, then said. "Maybe one or two."

"And it's nothing like little white lies." He tapped his fingers on the box, as if not wanting to open it but feeling its heft on his lap. "Like telling Ellie you were helping me this morning when we only started after lunch."

Norma winced. "True. But I didn't want to tell the story of Claudette and myself in bits and pieces. Ellie was dashing out and I want to get her opinion of my pen-pal before I start my tale."

"Will you tell *me* about Claudette?"

"Of course!" Norma nudged him with her elbow. "But first, let's open the mystery box."

"And watch Star Wars," he joked.

"Tonight, tomorrow, whenever," Norma said, matching his joking tone. "And by the way, this box is beautiful. You'll have to show Quinn when he gets home. Maybe he'll consider making smaller items for his business."

It was oak, scuffed at the corners, with a brass latch darkened by age. A rusty lock stood in their way. "Best not to put it off," she said, brushing her hair back with the back of her hand. "If it's been waiting this long, it can wait no longer."

Graham rubbed his palms on his jeans, staring at it as though it might reveal its secrets without needing to be opened.

"But you don't have to look," Norma said gently, settling back beside him. "You could shove it under the bed. Pretend it's not there."

He gave a small, humorless laugh. "That's exactly what I've been doing for years."

Norma ran a hand lightly across the dark wood, skirting the antique metal corners, and tracing the initials on the lid.

"D.B. Duncan Brody. That's my dad." Graham brushed the carving, as if clearing the letters of dust.

"Boy, your family is just as Scottish as Quinn's family with the names." Norma tapped the lock. "Do you have the key?"

Graham shook the lock. He frowned. "No. And it's a beauty. I don't want to break it open."

Norma grabbed her purse from the table and pulled out a thin leather pouch. She unzipped it and displayed the thin tools within. "I'll give it a try."

Graham's eyes shot open. "Are you also a lock picker? What else can you do?"

Norma grinned and pulled a chair in front of them. She motioned for him to put the box on it. "I'm not guaranteeing anything, but I got pretty good at picking locks when I was young."

"Why would a child need to have that skill?"

"Diaries." Norma licked her lips and squinted at the lock before choosing a slim pick. "I upgraded from using bobby pins in my teens. Here we go."

For the next five minutes, Graham left her in peace. He didn't move a muscle but watched the various emotions cross her face; concentration, frustration, hope, and finally joy.

"Dang, I'm good," Norma chortled as she flicked the lock open and handed it with a flourish to Graham. "Your mystery box awaits you, sir."

He shook his head. "Norma, you never fail to amaze me."

"May the amazing feats continue for years to come," Norma said, grinning with delight. "Come on, come on. Open the dang thing."

He lifted the lid carefully and rested it against the back of the chair. The lid creaked. Inside, neatly packed, lay fragments of another man's life: his father's, preserved in silence.

The first thing Graham lifted out was a stack of photographs, their edges curling, the kind of pictures that smelled faintly of vinegar and dust. He shuffled through them carefully. There were black-and-white shots of his father as a boy in shorts too big for him, his knees knobby and bare. A few from his teenage years: gangly, leaning against a car with friends, cigarette dangling with the effort of trying to look older.

"That's your dad?" Norma leaned closer.

"Yeah," Graham said softly. He tapped one photo, where his father squinted against the sun, standing by a lake. "I've never seen this one. He looks—different. Happier."

"And is this you?" Norma pointed to a picture of his father holding a baby, a huge grin on his face.

"It is," Graham paused, head tilted as if soaking in the image. "I've never seen this one either."

They set the photos aside. Next was a watch: a heavy vintage piece, the leather strap cracked, but the face still gleaming faintly in the light. Graham turned it in his palm, the weight of it unexpectedly comforting. He remembered his father's wrist, broad and capable, but never this watch. "I don't think I've ever seen him wear it," he murmured.

"Maybe it was for best days only," Norma suggested. "Some things aren't for everyday. They're for when you want to remember who you are."

Beneath the watch lay a cigarette lighter, its silver casing inlaid with mother-of-pearl. The design caught the light in shifting rainbows. Graham snapped it open; the wheel still turned, though no flame appeared.

Norma whistled. "That's not the kind you buy at a corner store."

"No," Graham said. His father hadn't smoked in his memory. "Maybe it was a gift. Or maybe..." He trailed off, shrugging. "Another life."

They lifted out a small leather pouch of old coins, some foreign, some local but from decades past. He shook them into his hand; the jingle was sharp, almost musical.

But at the very bottom, tucked flat against the wood, was an envelope. Thick, yellowed, marked in dark ink with French words Graham's schoolroom memory only half-understood:

Pour tes yeux seulement – Lucien.

He said the words aloud, clumsy. "What does it mean?"

"Roughly translated, it means for your eyes only," Norma said.

"And... Lucien. A name, I guess. But..." He shook his head. "I've never heard it before. Not once."

The envelope seemed heavier than its size. He slid a finger beneath the flap, heart thumping, and drew out a sheaf of letters tied with a ribbon brittle as autumn leaves. And between the pages, folded carefully, was a single photograph: a boy, black-and-white, standing stiffly in front of a farmhouse. His hair was combed neatly, his shoes polished, but his eyes were dark, solemn, too old for his face, looking straight into the camera.

Graham stared. "Who is this?"

Norma leaned closer. "Could be your dad, couldn't it? As a child?"

"No," Graham said immediately. He knew his father's boyhood face from the other photos, the curve of his ears, the stubborn set of his jaw. But this child *did* have the same jaw.

The farmhouse behind the boy looked foreign somehow, not the architecture he knew from growing up in New Brunswick. The shutters, the steep roof, the crooked stones in the wall, older, European. He set the picture down carefully. The letters trembled in his hand.

"Are you going to read one?" Norma asked softly.

"I don't know if I should," Graham admitted. "It feels like spying. Like this was meant for Lucien alone."

She gave him a steady look. "Then why would your father keep them? Why not burn them, or throw the whole envelope away? He left it for someone to find. Maybe for you."

Graham swallowed. The paper smelled faintly musty as he untied the ribbon. The handwriting was elegant, slanted, in French again.

His grasp of the language was too shaky to follow every word, but he caught fragments: *mon petit garçon ... je suis désolé.*

Norma flipped through the letters and stopped abruptly. "Who is Stuart Brody?"

Graham jerked in surprise. "That's my grandfather. Why?"

Norma waved the letter at him. "Because he's mentioned in this letter."

Graham raised a hand. "Nope, nope. Nothing more tonight, if you please. I'll never be able to sleep." He picked up the photograph again, staring at the boy's eyes. "Do you think he's a relation of mine? I've never heard of a French connection before."

Norma touched his hand lightly. "Could be. Sometimes families bury things too deep. But they don't disappear. They wait. Like this box."

He let out a shaky breath. "Do you think... do you think I should try to find out who he was? Who Lucien was?"

"I think you have to with your grandfather's name mentioned," she said simply. "Otherwise, it'll haunt you." Her tone was practical, but her eyes were warm. "And you don't have to do it alone. We could get the Heritage Harvesters together. You know they'd love this sort of mystery; old photos, hidden letters, family secrets. It's right up their alley."

Graham smiled. The Heritage Harvesters, the seniors genealogy group he and Norma were a part of, and who Ellie was teaching how to write their memoirs, had solved family mysteries before, tracking down forgotten land deeds, piecing together town lore from attic finds. But this was different. This might be blood, family, something that might change his very sense of who he was.

"Yes," he said slowly. "Maybe you're right. Maybe that's the best way."

Norma squeezed his hand once, then let go. "Then let's do it. We'll gather the gang tomorrow morning at the Cozy Corner Café, have some of Maggie's delicious pastries, drink some tea, bring out the letters, and start pulling at the threads. Sooner or later, something will unravel. And we'll keep the introduction to the Star Wars universe for another time."

Graham closed the box carefully, the envelope of Lucien's letters resting on top. The weight of the mystery pressed on him, but for the first time since opening it, he felt less alone.

Outside, the sun was setting, gilding the edges of the tiny house with gold. Inside, the shadows lengthened, and the memory box waited, no longer silent, but whispering of stories yet to be uncovered.

Chapter Three

The glass doors of Charles de Gaulle airport slid open with a hiss, and the smell of jet fuel was replaced with something subtler: early morning city air. Ellie stepped through them as if walking through a threshold into a long-awaited dream. Paris. The city she'd only visited through books, lectures, and distant stories.

Next to her, Quinn shouldered his bag and pulled hers, a half-smile twitching at the corner of his lips as he looked at the sea of taxi cabs waiting outside. "You're already taking mental notes, aren't you?"

Ellie turned to him, brushing her dark hair out of her face. "Notes?"

"For that lecture you'll give when we're back home. 'My Family Lineage in France: A Journey Across Time.' I can already see the PowerPoint slides."

She smirked, nudging him playfully. "You mock me, monsieur, but this city holds the beginning of everything."

"The beginning of our honeymoon," he said, reaching for her hand.

That shut her up in the best way.

They slid into a white taxi, the driver confirming the address of their hotel. As the car joined the stream of traffic, Ellie leaned her forehead against the window. Paris glowed like it had already lived in her blood for centuries. Narrow streets with ironwork balconies, wide boulevards with golden statues, riverside booksellers and garden gates. Every corner felt like an unopened book beckoning her to come explore.

Her fingers fumbled for the leather-bound notebook in her satchel. She opened it to the back page where she had taped a printed copy of the Ethier family tree she had painstakingly created through the years. The name she always paused over: Léonard Ethier, 1633–1689. Born in France. Emigrated to Quebec in 1665. Shoemaker.

He had been the seed of their line in the New World. And beyond that, she had nothing.

Quinn noticed. "Thinking about the shoemaker again?"

Ellie nodded. "He left everything. His country, family... There's no record of why."

Quinn's voice softened. "Maybe he just wanted to build something new."

Ellie looked out the window again. "Or maybe something chased him out."

***

The Cozy Corner Café had always been the Heritage Harvesters genealogy group's unofficial headquarters. They'd been meeting here every Wednesday for close to two years, always welcomed by Ellie's best friend, Maggie, who constantly delighted them with new pastries and warm smiles. The back room round table was reserved for them, and Maggie always had a plate or two of cookies or muffins ready, along with as many pots of tea needed.

This particular unscheduled meeting felt different. The September sun warmed the pavement outside, but the café was cool, its ceiling fans turning lazily above the tables. The air smelled of cinnamon and nutmeg from the morning's batch of scones, mingling with the earthy bitterness of fresh coffee. The café's soundtrack was a gentle blend of soft jazz and the clink of ceramic mugs.

Virginia sat at her usual spot near the door, beside her childhood friend, Norma. She always took the same seat, part habit, part practicality, since it gave her a view of both the entrance and the counter. She was a people watcher. She moved with a deliberate grace, the kind that came from a lifetime of pacing oneself while raising a family. Her cardigan sleeves were pushed up slightly, revealing thin wrists and a delicate Longines watch her late husband had given her on their fortieth wedding anniversary.

Around her, the other members of the group were settling in. Norma had already spread her binder open in front of her, a clean page ready, pen placed neatly beside it. Her t-shirt of choice this day was a vintage Star Trek showing Spock and Captain Kirk, phasers at the ready. She loved her sci-fi. Phil was still fussing with his laptop bag, muttering under his breath about a zipper determined to jam at exactly the wrong moment.

Across the table, Ruth, her husband Jeremy, and her sister Shirley were fixing their cups of tea, all wondering what the urgent meeting was all about. Especially one where Ellie wasn't involved. But Norma had sounded excited when she called everyone, and they were eager for a new mystery to dig into.

Virginia took a quiet breath. She'd rehearsed what she wanted to say in her head on the walk over, but the reality of saying it was heavier than she'd expected. She glanced toward the counter, where Maggie was pulling a shot of espresso for a customer, and then back to her friends. "I suppose," she began, her voice gentle but carrying enough authority to cut through the hum of conversation, "I should tell you all something important before we dive into Graham's mystery."

The words had the intended effect. Conversations stopped, heads turned, and even Maggie glanced in their direction at the abrupt silence before returning to the espresso machine.

Norma, who had been writing the title "Graham's Mystery" at the top of a page, stopped and looked up sharply. "What's going on, Ginny?"

Virginia smiled faintly at the nickname; it was a piece of shared history, a reminder of their friendship as girls, meeting at Virginia's family campground, and all the adventures they'd had together each summer. "I'm leaving the Tiny House Haven Community," she said, her fingers tightening imperceptibly around her mug. "I'll be moving in with my daughter north of Toronto."

The air at the table changed, as though someone had just opened a door to let in a draft. Conversations from the rest of the café faded into the background.

"You're leaving?" Norma asked, the disbelief in her tone tempered by something softer, almost vulnerable.

"Yes." Virginia kept her voice steady, though her heart was thudding faster than she'd anticipated. "It's time, Norma. The tiny house has been a wonderful change for me, and I've loved these months with you again, but I miss my family more than I thought I would. My daughter has been asking me for years to come live with her, and I think... well, this is the right time."

Norma's lips pressed together, her fingers curling around her coffee cup. She was a woman who prided herself on being practical, but practicality didn't erase the sting of losing a friend to distance. "I understand," she said finally, her tone quiet now. "I just, well, selfishly, I don't want to imagine the group without you. Or the Haven without you, for that matter. Who's going to sit on the porch with me and watch the fireflies?"

Virginia's chuckle was warm but tinged with nostalgia. "You'll still watch fireflies, my dear. You'll just have to do it with someone else occasionally." She glanced over at Graham, caught his eye, and winked. Graham blushed.

Phil had been silent until now, processing the news. He leaned forward, resting his forearms on the table. "Virginia, I'll miss you too, but I can't fault you for choosing family. That's something you can't get back if you miss it."

Virginia turned to him, her expression softening. “I knew you’d understand, Phil. And actually… you’re part of the reason I feel comfortable about leaving.”

Phil’s brows furrowed. “Me?”

“Yes,” Virginia said, the faintest smile tugging at the corners of her mouth. “When I spoke with Sara this week, I asked her if she could let you have my house.”

The effect on Phil was immediate: surprise, followed by cautious hope. “You mean… take over your lease?”

“Exactly,” Virginia replied. “You were scheduled to get a unit in two months, weren’t you?”

“That’s right. November.”

“Well, Sara agreed to let you move into mine as soon as I leave. No more waiting.”

Phil’s hand went to his newly grown goatee, buying time to think. “Virginia… that’s, well, that’s incredible. I don’t know how to thank you.”

“You can start by saying *thank you*,” Norma said with a teasing smile, though her eyes were bright with emotion.

Phil laughed softly. “Thank you, Virginia. Really. You’ve just made my year. I signed the papers yesterday to sell my house to a young couple, with the clause of me moving into the tiny house in November. They were anxious to take over the house, and now I can tell them it will be sooner than expected.” He trailed off, shaking his head as though still trying to believe it.

Virginia reached across the table to squeeze his hand. “It makes me happy to know the place will go to someone who values community.”

Around them, murmurs of approval passed through the group. Ruth leaned forward. “That’s a wonderful thing to do,” she said. “But we will all miss you, Virginia.”

Virginia smiled, but inside, the weight of leaving pressed on her. She thought of the early mornings when the fog hung low over the lake, the creak of the porch steps, the neighbor's cat who napped in her window box. She would miss those small, steady pieces of her life she had come to appreciate in such a short time. Yet the image of her daughter's kitchen; sunlight streaming in, the smell of bread, her granddaughter's piano practice in the background, was stronger.

Norma was thinking of those same quiet mornings at the Haven, but from her own perspective: turning up at Virginia's for a cup of tea on the porch, swapping stories until the mosquitoes came out. The idea of that porch sitting empty felt wrong, like a book missing from its shelf.

Phil's mind, meanwhile, was already racing with possibilities: if his desk would fit in the tiny space, how he might plant tomatoes in the spring in the communal garden. Having his friends close by.

Virginia took a sip of her tea and continued, "Sara said she'll make the paperwork easy for you, Phil. You can start moving in next week."

"That soon?" he asked.

"Yes," she said. "I didn't bring much from my old house, and some things are still in boxes. My daughter and her husband are coming with a moving truck. It just makes sense to hand the tiny house straight over."

Norma exhaled slowly, then straightened her shoulders. "Well, if that's the plan, I'll be there to help you pack. Someone's got to make sure you don't leave your family albums behind."

"I'd appreciate that," Virginia said warmly. "I'd trust no one else." She knew there'd be more talk than actual packing, but it would be the last time they'd be together for a while and Virginia looked forward to it.

The conversation drifted after that for a few moments. But the undercurrent of change was there, threading through each exchange. The laughter was genuine, but every so often, someone's gaze would linger on Virginia, as if committing her to memory in this familiar setting.

Chapter Four

Graham pushed the teak memory box into the middle of the table.

"Don't look so nervous," Norma whispered to him.

"I feel like I'm bringing my father's ghost into a room of strangers," Graham muttered.

"Not strangers," she corrected. "Friends who like nothing better than a ghost."

"I take it that whatever lies inside this box is the reason for this meeting?" Shirley asked, adjusting her glasses.

"It is," Norma said. "We've got a mystery for you. A family mystery."

Graham laid out the letters and the photograph on the table like evidence in a case. He explained what he knew; or rather, what he didn't know. "This envelope was in my father's box." He held it up so everyone could see the writing on the front. "They were all written by a woman named Emilie to her son, Lucien. Whoever this Lucien is, my dad never spoke about him. Never even mentioned his name. They were sent to my father, but I think they had something to do with my grandfather."

"The letters are all in French," Norma butted in. "So, we'll have to do some translating."

"Hand them out and let's see what we can do," Ruth said. "My French is shaky, but I'm sure we can use Google Translate for words we don't know."

"Or we could do the whole letter that way," Virginia suggested.

"I think this would be more personal," Norma said. "And we could all do with a little refresher in the language."

Graham handed out the letters, and for the next half hour they all worked diligently to transcribe Emilie's letters.

"Oh, heavens," Ruth whispered, as she and Jeremy finished their shared letter. She looked up at Graham and blinked quickly. "You never heard about this boy?"

"Not a word," Graham said.

"Is everyone finished?" Norma asked, looking to see everyone had put their pens down. "Let's read what we've got, starting with the earliest. That would be yours, Ruth."

Ruth sat straighter in her chair and gazed at the translation she had come up with. "This is the essence of the letter." She took a deep breath, gave Graham a slight smile, and started reading, faltering a couple of times.

Mon cher petit Lucien,

This morning I watched you sleeping in your crib, your cheeks rosy like autumn apples. My heart overflows when I think of you. Your father isn't here; he works far away from Baie-Saint-Paul, on the great rivers where they bring down the logs. It's a dangerous job, but he's courageous and wants us to want for nothing. When the wind whistles through the pines, I like to believe it's his voice greeting us. One day, when the river is calm, he'll come back to take you in his arms. Until then, I love you for both of us. Sleep soundly, my child, you are surrounded by love.

Your mother who adores you,

Émilie

"So," Norma said slowly. "We know for a fact Lucien is Emilie's son and that the father is off somewhere working."

"At least that's what she says," Shirley mumbled, garnering a sharp look from Ruth.

"Mine is next," said Phil.

My sweet boy,

Autumn covers the trees with gold and fire, and you're already running after leaves in the yard. How I wish your father could see that! He's gone to look for work on the railways. He wrote to me that with every nail he hammers, he thinks of you, that he's building for your future. Imagine, my little one, those great iron locomotives crossing forests and fields! One day, perhaps you'll travel on those rails and know that his labor still lives on. He never held your little hand, but in every thought, he holds you close to his heart.

With all my love, your mother

"Now he's working on the railroads," Shirley said, shaking her head. "Sounds fishy."

"Shirley!" Ruth said. "There's no need for commentary on something you don't know for a fact."

"Sorry," Shirley said, looking down at her page. "Mine is the next one."

My little treasure,

Winter has arrived. The snow covers our village like a silent, white blanket. I think of your father, in the logging camps, wielding the axe and the saw. He once told me that each plank sent to town was like a silent letter from him. He is a strong man, as solid as the tall fir trees. When I see you fearlessly climbing onto chairs, I recognize his spirit within you. You have his bravery, Lucien, and that reassures me. Even if he can't tuck you in at night, his love is sewn into each of my stories. You are never alone, my child.

All days, your mother

Norma held up a hand as Shirley looked to add a comment. "Yes, we realize he is now back logging. No need to say more. The next letter is mine."

My darling Lucien,

The lilacs fill the garden with their scent, and you run among the flowers like a bird. Your father is still on the roads, traveling to find his place in this world. But in my memory, he is very close. He sang old songs with a sweet, clear voice, and sometimes, when you laugh, I think I hear them again. He was a man who carried hope wherever he went. He left me that hope, and I pass it on to you through my arms and kisses. When you raise your head to the sun, think that it is his luminous gaze that accompanies you.

With love, your mother

"Why do you think she felt the need to write these letters in the first place?" Virginia asked. "It's obvious the father is not around but she feels a need to create someone for her son."

"I have the last letter," Graham said. "It's dated January, 1898, so Lucien would have been about five. And I had to use Google."

My darling little boy,

When you read these words, I may no longer be here. My health is failing, and I no longer have the right to keep it a secret. The stories I told you about your father came from my desire to protect you, to fill your childhood with warmth. But it is time to tell you the truth. Your father's name is Stuart Brody. He was neither a log driver, nor a rail layer, nor a distant traveler. He was a doctor at the hospital. He was a good, gentle man, who laughed easily. We didn't have much time together, but he loved me, and from that love you were born. I didn't know I was pregnant when he left and he never knew about you. The day he left he said Emilie Tremblay, I will return for you one day, and I kept waiting. But he never did, and I have no idea why. Forgive my fables, my son. I only wanted you to grow up surrounded by his memory, however imperfect. Always remember: you are the child of a great love, and nothing could be truer.

Your mother who loves you forever, Émilie

Stunned silence as everyone took in what the letters revealed.

"So, your grandfather didn't even know he had a son," Shirley said. "And Emilie didn't know she was pregnant when he left."

"And she obviously didn't know how to get in touch with him," Virginia added.

"Because surely she would have let him know he had a son," Phil said, a slight tremor in his voice.

“Lucien was born of a great love,” Virginia said softly. “I wonder why he had to leave, and why he didn’t take her with him.”

"Or why he never came back," Norma muttered.

Graham remained silent, letting the conversation flow around him. “We may never know,” he finally said.

Norma sat forward, arms on the table, fingers tapping against the wood. “You do know she gave us two incredible pieces of information, right?” She waited till she had everyone’s attention. “She gave us her full name and where she lived, Baie-Saint-Paul!” Norma nudged Graham gently. “Show them the picture.”

He took the ragged edged photograph resting on the table and handed it first to Ruth, who studied it before passing it around.

Shirley adjusted the photograph closer to her. “Look at the boy’s eyes. You can tell he’s kin. That nose; same shape as yours, Graham.”

He blinked, startled. He hadn’t noticed the resemblance.

Phil was already pulling out his laptop, fingers flying. “All right, let’s start with the basics. What was your grandfather’s name?”

“Stuart,” Graham said. “Stuart Brody. Born around 1865 in Scotland. He came to Canada around 1890 and married my grandmother, Harriet, in 1894 in Halifax. My dad, Duncan was born in 1895.”

Phil typed rapidly. “Let’s check census records. Quebec archives might have something, especially if Lucien stayed there.”

Shirley squinted at the original letters. “This handwriting, see how careful it is? Almost like someone who didn’t want to make mistakes. Not a practiced writer. But heartfelt.”

It didn’t take Phil long. He tapped the keys, squinting at the screen. “Here we go. Quebec parish records, 1893. Baptism for a Lucien Tremblay. Father: unknown. Mother: Emilie Tremblay. Address listed as Baie-Saint-Paul.” He turned the screen to the group.

The record was there in neat script, undeniable.

"Wait," Jeremy held up a hand. "There could be more than one Lucien Tremblay with a mother named Emilie born at that time."

"But there were no other entries that popped up for those specific pieces of information," Phil said. There *are* other Lucien Tremblays, but not born then, and not with a mother named Emilie."

"Are we making an assumption?" Ruth asked. "Ellie would not be pleased."

"When does preponderance of evidence override assumptions?" Norma asked.

They all looked at each other, back at Phil, who shrugged, and then waited for Graham to say something.

Graham looked at his friends and nodded. "I think it's true. My grandfather had another child."

"With Emilie," Phil confirmed. "Since she never married Stuart. It seems more likely now that he left without ever knowing about Lucien. But Lucien was real."

Graham sat back heavily. "My dad never opened those letters. He must have thought they were just keepsakes from his father. Maybe even things he didn't want to know."

Norma's voice was gentle. "Or things he was afraid to know."

Jeremy tapped the table. "Stuart married in 1894. Lucien was born in 1893, so Stuart was single at the time."

"That makes it a bit easier to take," Graham said. "It would have been horrible had he already been married. I met my grandfather a couple of times when I was young. He was a funny man, deeply in love with my grandmother."

"How was he with your dad?" Norma asked softly.

Graham hesitated. "Pretty much like me and my dad."

"Fathers and sons," Phil mumbled. "Why is there always such tension there?"

The photograph of the boy, Lucien, stared up at them from the table. Suddenly he wasn't just a mystery. He was part of Graham's family.

Maggie came over with fresh pots of tea and laid a hand on her grandfather's shoulder. "This is almost exactly what happened with you and my grandmother, Octavie."

The group froze, not sure how Graham would react to being reminded of that fact. He took a deep breath and nodded. "It is indeed. If I had known your mother was my daughter, nothing would have kept me from her." He gave her hand a quick squeeze and turned back to his friends around the table. "Let's see what else we can find."

Phil shifted in his seat, as if uncomfortable with what he was about to say. "I'm going to make another assumption here, and I don't care what anyone says. I bet if Lucien had received these letters, he would have found your grandfather. So, something, or someone, didn't give them to him."

"But sent them to your grandfather instead," Norma said.

"But when, and why didn't he get in touch with Lucien?" Ruth asked.

Shirley huffed. "That's one thing about genealogy I absolutely hate. Not every question will have an answer."

"There's so much to look for," Ruth muttered.

"There is," Graham nodded. "But I really only wanted help with the letters at the moment."

"It's a bit overwhelming," Norma said with a quick look at him and then a raised eyebrow to the rest of the group.

"We certainly understand that," Shirley said. "Everyone has to proceed at their own pace."

Phil leaned forward, his voice firm. "But you do know your grandfather is connected to this family." He chuckled. "And don't forget DNA. These days, the dead practically email you."

Graham raised an eyebrow. "Funny you mention that. Maggie sent me one of those DNA kits a few months ago. Said it'd give me something to do while downsizing." He gave a wry smile. "I spit in the tube and mailed it off right away. Thought it'd be amusing to see how much of me is actually Scottish and how much is just stubborn."

Norma's eyes lit up. "Do you know what company it was?"

"Ancestry, I think."

"Oh, perfect. If the results come back soon, we can check for cousin matches. That might help narrow down this Lucien business."

Graham shrugged. "Wouldn't that be something. Imagine finding kin you never knew you had, just because you spit into a tube."

Phil tapped the table. "Trust me, stranger things happen every week in genealogy. That test may solve the mystery for us yet."

Having read the letters and tossed around ideas, Graham felt wrung out, but not alone. The Harvesters had gathered around him like a circle of lanterns, casting light into corners he hadn't dared look at on his own.

Norma slipped the photograph of Lucien back into its envelope. "You know what I think?" she said quietly.

"What?" Graham asked.

"I don't know how this information got to you, but someone wanted Lucien to be remembered, even if your dad or grandfather couldn't face it. That's why the letters stayed, waiting. Not for them, but for you."

Graham swallowed hard. "But what do I do with it? With him?"

She gave him a small, steady smile. "We keep looking. We dig. That's what we do. We'll find out what happened to Lucien and Emilie. And you'll give him his place in your family story."

He nodded slowly. He held the box between his hands. It felt heavier now, but in a different way; less like a burden, more like a responsibility.

For the first time since opening it, he felt something close to peace.

The boy in the photograph would not be forgotten.

***

The Cozy Corner Café seemed to hold them in a golden pause, the scent of cinnamon and coffee wrapping around them like a quilt. Outside, life went on: delivery trucks rumbled past, a cyclist rang his bell, and somewhere down the street, a dog barked. Inside, the Heritage Harvesters sat together, already adjusting to the idea that their little constellation was about to shift.

The meeting was winding down with small talk. Virginia found herself half-listening to the conversations around her, her mind slipping toward lists of what to pack, and what to give away. The quilt on her bed, her mother's, was coming, of course. The mismatched mugs could stay or be given away.

Phil, sitting to her right, kept jotting notes in the margins of his genealogy binder, though his thoughts were miles away. In his head, he was arranging what furniture might fit in the tiny living room, picturing where the sunlight would hit in the mornings. He kept sneaking glances at Virginia, silently hoping he'd be able to make the house feel as alive as she had.

Norma was perhaps the only one in the group who wasn't distracted by her own mental lists. She watched Virginia closely, memorizing the way her friend's cardigan bunched at the elbows, the way she stirred her tea without looking. Norma had known other people who'd moved away, life had a way of shifting the pieces, but Virginia's absence would leave a hollowness that would take more than time to fill. She had been surprised how easily they had molded into each other's lives after finding each other again. And she was thankful for this short time they had experienced together later in life.

By noon, the café was beginning to fill with the lunch crowd. The group started stacking their papers, shutting laptops, and packing bags. A few people drifted off early with promises to get in touch with ideas and solutions for Graham's mystery. That left just three of them, Virginia, Norma, and Phil, still at the large table in the back room.

"You two staying for lunch?" Phil asked, glancing toward the chalkboard menu. "Maggie's got a special ham and cheese croissant today."

Virginia smiled. "Tempting, but I should probably get back. My daughter is calling this afternoon to go over the moving schedule."

Norma gave Phil a pointed look. "I think we should at least walk her home. Make sure she doesn't float away."

Virginia laughed softly. "I'm not as fragile as you think, Norma."

"No," Norma said, "but you're important. There's a difference."

They lingered long enough for Phil to grab another coffee to go and for Norma to tuck her binder into her tote. The three of them stepped outside into the brightness of the day. The air was slightly warmer, the sky an unbroken blue, and the faint scent of Chrysanthemums and Goldenrod drifted around them.

They walked slowly, falling into the kind of companionable silence only close friendships allow. At the end of the path behind the Cozy Corner Café, where it turned into the main road for the Tiny House Haven Community, Virginia stopped.

"I want to thank you both," she said, looking from one to the other. "Not just for today, for everything. These past months at the Haven, meeting and being accepted so kindly into this group... they've been some of the happiest of my life."

Norma's throat tightened, but she managed a small smile. "You're not gone yet. And when you are, I expect letters. Not emails, letters."

Virginia nodded. "Letters, then. And video chats for meetings when I'm not helping out with my grandkids." Her face lit up at the thought.

Phil cleared his throat. "I'll take good care of your place, Virginia. You have my word. And if you ever want to visit, you're more than welcome."

The three of them stood there for a moment, the summer sounds of the Tiny House Haven around them; Gerry, Sara's handyman, mowing the grass around the beach at the lake, children laughing in the distance as they dashed onto the hiking paths leading into the forest and their parents calling out to them to slow down. It was an ordinary scene, but it shimmered with the knowledge that this was one of the last times they'd all walk home together from a meeting.

Finally, Virginia adjusted her cardigan sleeves and smiled. "Alright. Enough standing in the street looking sentimental. Let's get moving before Norma insists on buying me lunch anyway."

Norma chuckled, and they resumed walking. The road to the house wasn't long, but each step seemed to stretch, as if the Haven itself was reluctant to let her go. When they reached the little gate leading to Virginia's tidy front walk, she paused again.

"I'll expect you, Norma, this evening for tea and star gazing," she said.

Norma nodded. "I'll see you then."

Virginia patted Phil's arm. "And Phil, come by any time to take measurements. It'll be helpful for you to have an idea where everything can go."

Phil gave a little salute. "That would be helpful and much appreciated. Are you available in the morning?"

Chapter Five

By the time Ellie and Quinn had checked in, left their luggage in their room and reached the rooftop terrace of their hotel for a late breakfast, the day had started for most Parisians. Ellie sank into her seat at a wrought iron table and craned her neck to see the view beyond the terrace's see-through fence. The Eiffel Tower shimmered in the distance as the temperatures began to rise, just visible between the roofs. Haughty looking pigeons flew from the tops of various buildings, their wings catching the morning sun, their coos ebbing and flowing.

Their waiter brought a menu, but Ellie couldn't stop staring at the view. Not just of the city, but of Quinn; his messy hair tousled from travel, the slight beard shadow that always grew too fast, his shirt wrinkled but complimenting the light blue of his eyes.

"You're staring," he said without looking up from the menu.

"You look like someone who belongs in a black-and-white film."

He met her eyes and smiled. "And you look like someone who's halfway into another century."

Ellie laughed, surprised by the accuracy. "You're not wrong."

As they sipped water, she took a breath. "Are you sure you don't mind going to Rivièreclaire? This is supposed to be *our* honeymoon, not a genealogy research trip."

Quinn raised an eyebrow. "Before we met, I didn't think much about my ancestors. I was fully living in the present."

"And now?"

"Now, I find myself wondering what my grandfather did before he met my grandmother." He lowered his menu and gave her his full attention. "I'm curious about who I'm from."

"So are your sisters."

He nodded. "There is that. Fiona sent me an email before we left. I'll show you later. But she's really excited about something she found and will send more information when we get back."

"It's an addicting hobby," Ellie said with a knowing smile.

"Actually being able to visit the place your ancestors lived will be fascinating. I think I'm looking forward to it as much as you are." He returned to his menu. "You think we'll find something there?"

"I don't know," she said honestly. "But I'd like to try."

Quinn nodded slowly. "I've always wanted to go on a high-speed train, so that'll be a new experience. We'll take our time."

Ellie smiled. "Deal."

They clinked glasses in agreement.

"But after we eat, I desperately need a shower and a nap," he grumbled, rubbing his chin and wincing at the stubble. "I must look a mess."

"No worse than I do," she laughed, self-consciously running a hand through her hair. Yup, definitely needed a good brushing.

He glanced at his watch. "Do you think eleven is too early to visit your aunt's friend, Claudette?"

"If she's anything like Aunt Norma and the gang, she's already up and starting her day." Ellie grinned at the thought, gazing once again at the Eiffel Tower. "Did you know there are 1,665 stairs to the top of the Eiffel Tower."

"Oh, no," Quinn moaned.

Ellie held up a hand. "But you can only climb 674 of them to the second floor, and then you have to take the elevator?"

"Someone's been doing some research."

"We need to get our tickets in advance so we don't wait in a line," she said.

Quinn pulled out his phone and made the reservations. Taking extra time, he looked for a place to stay in Rivièreclaire and booked them a room in a small B&B.

***

Each part of the city they passed through delighted Ellie. The wide boulevards lined with sycamore trees felt different from the narrower streets she and Quinn had wandered as they left their hotel. There was a sense of history here, a hush that clung to the facades of old stone buildings. They were elegant without shouting about it; balconies with iron railings, flower boxes spilling with geraniums, doors painted in glossy enamel.

She checked the address scribbled on the note her Aunt Norma had given her before she left. The handwriting was instantly recognizable: bold loops, impatient slashes. *Put this into Claudette's hands. Not the postman, not a neighbor, not her concierge. Her hands.*

Now, standing before the carved oak door of a building that must have been erected during the Belle Époque, Ellie clutched the envelope and glanced at Quinn. He stood beside her, straight-backed, hands tucked into the pockets of his jeans, his expression unreadable as usual.

"You ready?" she asked, a little nervous.

Quinn gave a single nod. His scar, the thin jagged line curving from his temple down toward his jaw, caught the morning light. It always seemed to shift in mood depending on how people reacted to it; sometimes a badge, sometimes a shadow.

They caught the door as someone left the building and climbed to the second floor. The hallway was long with only two doors, each halfway down the hall. Ellie double checked the address, found the right door, and pressed the brass bell. The sound echoed inside.

A moment later, footsteps approached. The door opened, revealing a tall young woman whose presence immediately commanded the space. She looked as though she'd stepped straight from the glossy pages of a fashion magazine; long legs, narrow hips, dark hair swept into a careless knot only someone with perfect bone structure could make look effortless. She wore a pale cream silk blouse tucked into high-waisted black trousers, a severe look on anyone else but regal on her.

Her eyes, sharp and assessing, flicked from Ellie to Quinn to the envelope in Ellie's hands. "Oui?" she said, her voice crisp.

"Um—hello. I'm looking for Madame Claudette. I have a package for her from my Aunt Norma."

At the name, the young woman's expression changed slightly, though not enough to be welcoming. Her brows arched. "And you are?"

"Ellie. Ellie McLellan."

There was a pause, during which the young woman seemed to measure the weight of Ellie's presence, as though deciding whether she was worthy of admission. Ellie was used to this sort of scrutiny, though it rarely felt so piercing.

Finally, the woman stepped aside with a flick of her hand. "Come in."

The apartment was breathtaking. The foyer opened into a grand room that seemed to stretch forever. Sunlight spilled through tall windows draped in sheer linen curtains, catching on gilded mirrors and crystal vases. The walls were lined with bookshelves crammed with volumes in French and English, as well as countless sketchbooks stacked in precarious towers. The faint smell of citrus hung in the air, mixed with the sharper scent of fabric dye and freshly pressed cotton.

To the right, Ellie glimpsed a large workroom where bolts of fabric leaned like soldiers against the wall, and a cutting table was strewn with scissors, measuring tapes, and half-pinned garments on mannequins. A few young women moved about quietly, some sketching, some stitching, their concentration absolute.

The grandeur of the apartment was unmistakable, but there was also an intimacy to it; the lived-in clutter of someone who worked fiercely and passionately in the same space where they lived.

The tall young woman led them to the left and into an airy salon. Her movements were elegant, almost too deliberate, as though she was always aware of being watched. "Grandmère," she called in French. "Visitors for you."

From a corner near the window, a chair creaked. Ellie's eyes adjusted to see a plump woman rising slowly from a wheelchair. She was not tall, perhaps five foot four, but she carried herself with a presence that filled the room. Her cheeks were round, her smile warm but cautious. Her hair, silver threaded with remnants of brown, was styled in soft waves that framed her face. She wore a navy dress with a scattering of embroidered flowers across the bodice.

"Ah," she said in accented English, her voice both cheery and wary. "You must be Norma's niece. She sent me a message you'd be coming." She turned to the young woman. "And this is my granddaughter, Simone."

Ellie nodded at Simone and stepped forward quickly to the older woman. "I'm Ellie McLellan. And this is my husband, Quinn Walsh." They all shook hands and Ellie marveled at how strong Claudette's handshake was. She offered the envelope. "From Aunt Norma. She said to give it directly into your hands."

Claudette's eyes twinkled as she accepted it, holding it against her chest as though it were something precious, or dangerous. "Norma. Always bossy. Always precise. I should not be surprised."

Simone, meanwhile, had gone very still. Her gaze moved from Ellie to Quinn, and it lingered, too long, too intently, on the scar across his face. Her lips parted slightly, curiosity flickering across her features in a way that was neither subtle nor polite.

Quinn, as always, betrayed nothing. He stood with an air of detached patience, letting the scrutiny wash over him.

Claudette noticed at once. She clicked her tongue sharply. "Simone! Do not stare. It is rude."

Simone blinked, startled out of her trance. A faint flush colored her cheeks.

Quinn's mouth quirked into the barest suggestion of a smile. "It's all right. I'm used to it."

"No," Ellie interjected firmly. She placed a hand lightly on his arm. "It's not just a scar, it's a story. Quinn got it while working as a police officer in Scotland."

That seemed to break the spell. Simone's eyes widened, then softened. She drew in a breath, as if absorbing not just the information but the weight behind it. "My apologies," she said quietly. Her English, Ellie noticed, was flawless; crisp vowels, clean consonants, not a trace of hesitation. "I did not mean to be impolite."

Quinn nodded his head in acceptance.

Simone straightened, smoothing her blouse. "I will bring tea." She moved gracefully toward the kitchen.

Claudette chuckled. "She has the highest grades in her class, in English especially. She will pretend she is not proud, but I am proud enough for both of us." She moved to a couch and eased down, motioning for them to take the chairs across from her. "Sit, sit. Let's be comfortable."

When Simone returned moments later with a silver tray balanced easily in her hands, her composure had returned. "We always have a pot on the stove. Lucky us." She poured tea with the elegance of someone raised in a household where presentation mattered. Cups were distributed, sugar offered, biscuits set out. Then she seated herself quietly beside her grandmother, her eyes attentive.

Ellie felt the shift immediately. The hauteur Simone had worn at the door had dissolved into something else: curiosity, perhaps even eagerness.

Claudette sipped her tea. "Norma has written me letters for ... mon Dieu, how long? Nearly sixty years. She has bullied me into many things during that time, but now she bullies me into writing my memoir."

"Memoir?" Simone's head lifted.

"Yes." Claudette sighed, though her eyes sparkled. "She insists my stories must not be lost. She says my life is interesting. I say it is only *my* life."

Ellie leaned forward. "Aunt Norma never mentioned you before. She said she wanted to keep you to herself but she would explain when I got home. She's become very insistent on documenting her own life, so I can see how she'd want you to do the same. You might want to tell her you've started, or she might fly over here and dictate them herself."

Claudette laughed, her plump shoulders shaking. "That sounds like her, yes."

Simone glanced between them. "May I ask, if Grandmère is to share her memoir with your aunt, could she... perhaps... join your group?"

Ellie blinked. "Group?"

"Yes. I overheard one of their conversations when they were discussing the ... what was the name of the group?"

"The Heritage Harvesters?" Claudette supplied.

"Oui, c'est ca," Simone grinned, then faltered as she realized her grandmother was staring at her. "I heard nothing else, Grandmère, I swear."

Claudette patted her hand. "I have nothing to hide, Simone. I'm surprised you're interested in this."

Ellie smiled. "Yes, you mean our circle of writers and storytellers. I'm sure Aunt Norma has filled you in on that as well." She sent Claudette a smile. "We usually meet together, plus a couple of friends join by video chat. Your grandmother would be more than welcome."

"And me?" Simone's voice was careful, almost tentative, though her posture remained perfectly poised.

"You too," Ellie said warmly. "We'd be delighted to have both of you."

Simone's cheeks turned pink again. She ducked her head, almost shy for the first time since Ellie had met her.

Claudette gave a mock-groan. "You both sound like Norma! She bullies, you persuade, but it is the same result. I am trapped."

Ellie laughed. "Trapped into telling stories that deserve to be remembered."

Simone's gaze softened as she looked at her grandmother. "Grandmère has many stories about the war. Some she will not tell me. But I think, even if no one reads them while she is alive, they must be written. So they are not lost."

Ellie nodded. "I agree completely."

Claudette looked from her granddaughter to Ellie, her expression a mix of exasperation and affection. Then she shook her head, smiling ruefully. "Norma has found allies, I see."

The room went quiet for a moment, the kind of silence that hums with meaning. Outside, a breeze drifted through the window and rustled the curtains. The city's faint noises floated in, distant car horns, the chatter of pedestrians.

Claudette leaned back into the cushions of the couch, the envelope from Norma still resting on her lap. She hadn't opened it yet, and Ellie had the sense she was procrastinating. Perhaps she knew what it was, and it carried too much weight to be opened casually with company watching.

"You must think this apartment is too much for a woman like me," Claudette said suddenly, gesturing at the high ceiling, the gilded cornices, the rows of oil paintings and framed sketches that lined the walls. Her tone was light, but her eyes were sharp.

Ellie blinked. "It's beautiful," she said truthfully. "But not too much. It feels... earned."

Claudette chuckled, the sound warm but edged with something else. "Earned, perhaps. But not by me, not at first." She reached for her teacup, her fingers steady despite the slight stiffness in her movements. "This place, these rooms, it was my husband's doing. Jacques. He had a gift for seeing value where others saw only dust."

Simone looked up from her tea, her expression softening. "Grandpère was clever," she said simply.

"Clever, yes. Shrewd." Claudette's eyes grew distant, remembering. "After the war, when Paris was in ruins, when everyone was desperate to survive rather than to dream, Jacques began to buy. Small things at first. Shops, warehouses, buildings no one wanted because they were scarred by bombs or burdened with debt. He would repair them just enough, rent them out, sell them at a profit, then move on to the next. He never gambled. He only bought what others overlooked, and always with his own two eyes, never trusting the word of another man. By the 1960s he had done well enough to buy this apartment. Not for show, but for safety. For me, for Simone's father, for our family."

She swept her hand around, as though to encompass not just the room but the history embedded in it: the parquet floors polished by generations, the marble fireplace veined with green, the wrought-iron balconies that looked out over the broad boulevard below.

"It is large, yes," Claudette admitted. "Too large for one woman now. But Jacques said once a home should be like a coat: a little too big, so you have room to grow into it. He believed one must always leave space for possibility. And this is where my dreams came alive, my first collection was created in this very room."

Ellie let her eyes wander again, seeing the apartment anew; not just as a showpiece, but as a shelter built by foresight. The salon opened into a dining room with a long oak table scarred by decades of meals and debates. They had seen the workroom as they came in, spilling with color and texture, life sewn into every corner. In the far corridor were doors that must lead to the bedrooms that had once been filled with family voices. Even the air seemed touched by memory.

"There are people who help me keep it alive," Claudette continued. "Too many rooms for me to dust or air myself, so I have Brigette, who has been with us since before Simone was born, and Étienne, who handles the errands and makes sure the little repairs are seen to. And, of course, the girls in the workroom; students, apprentices. They think they come here only to learn fashion, but they also learn how to live in a place like this, how to make a home breathe instead of grow stale."

Simone smirked faintly. "Grandmère forgets she also has me, though I am treated more like another assistant than a granddaughter."

Claudette gave her a mock-stern glance. "You are spoiled and you know it. I let you use my fabrics when you design, and my mannequins, and sometimes even my scissors, though you always leave them in the wrong drawer."

A small laugh went around the room, but Ellie found herself glancing at Quinn, who was looking at the ornate plasterwork on the ceiling with a kind of detached appreciation. She wondered what he thought of it all.

Claudette must have sensed the question in Ellie's mind, for she leaned forward slightly and said, "It is easy to imagine a woman like me was born into such a place, no? But no. When the bombs fell, I was a girl who owned nothing but the shoes on my feet, and even those were patched. This," she gestured around again, "is what survival, patience, and Jacques' sharp eye built from the rubble."

Her tone grew softer. "I can walk slowly, yes, with pain. But mostly I am in the chair. That was the price of one bad day in the war. Jacques carried me through the rest of it, in more ways than one. So, this apartment is not just stone and wood. It is his devotion, laid out in square meters."

The words settled in the air like dust motes glittering in the sunlight.

Ellie felt a sudden, unexpected pang of gratitude, awe, and something tender she couldn't quite name. She looked at Simone, who was staring at her grandmother with a mixture of pride and defiance, as though daring anyone to underestimate the woman before them.

"Thank you for telling us," Ellie said softly. "It makes the place feel even more alive."

Claudette gave a small shrug, but her eyes were shining. "Norma would scold me if I did not. She always says I must not pretend to be less than I am. She says false modesty is boring."

Quinn finally spoke, his voice low. "Sounds like she was right."

Claudette beamed at him, and even Simone seemed to approve of his comment.

The tea had grown cold in their cups, but no one seemed to notice. Conversation had drifted into silences that weren't uncomfortable, just full of possibility. Ellie caught Simone watching her grandmother again; expectant, almost hungry, as though waiting for a door to open.

"Grandmère," Simone said softly, "perhaps you can tell them one story. Just a little one."

Claudette's plump hands folded over the envelope from Norma, and she let out a slow sigh. "You see, Ellie? This is how they trap me. First Norma, now Simone. I am ambushed on all sides."

"You don't have to," Ellie said quickly, though her heart leapt at the idea.

"I know." Claudette tilted her head, a smile tugging at her lips. "But perhaps I want to."

She reached for her cane and shifted in her chair, as if steadying herself before a performance. Her voice, when she began, was not theatrical but measured, deliberate.

"It was in '44. The Allies were close, but no one knew how close, and the Germans were everywhere still. I was fifteen. My brother Henri and I, he was only thirteen, were sent to fetch bread from a baker who would trade with us. We walked through streets that were not streets anymore, only rubble and smoke. We thought we were clever, we knew which alleys to take, which corners to avoid. But we were not clever enough."

Her gaze had grown far away, into the past, but her voice stayed steady.

"There was a raid that morning. Not on soldiers, on civilians. Planes flew so low I swore I could see the whites of the pilot's eyes. The ground shook, buildings fell. Henri pushed me into a doorway just as the bombs came down. The wall collapsed on us. Only one of us came out."

Her hand drifted to her hip, her leg, as if reminding herself of the cost. "That is why I walk like an old woman now, and even when I was young. That is why sometimes I do not walk at all. They pulled me out hours later, and the first thing I saw was Jacques, though I did not know him yet. He was not a soldier, not a doctor. Just a man with strong arms and a stubborn will. He carried me to the truck that took the wounded to safety. Later, he came to visit me. Again, and again. That is how we began."

The room was silent except for the ticking of an ornate clock on the mantel.

Ellie felt her throat tighten. She glanced at Quinn, who was watching Claudette with the quiet respect of someone who knew what it meant to carry scars invisible as well as visible. Simone, though, sat utterly still, her dark eyes shining, her chin lifted proudly even as her lips trembled.

"That is only one story," Claudette said at last, her voice breaking the spell. She smiled faintly. "And Norma insists there are many. She is right, but..." She exhaled, as though releasing a burden. "It is not easy. You open the door to one memory, and the whole house of them comes crashing in."

Simone leaned forward, touching her grandmother's hand gently. "That is why you must write them down, Grandmère. So they will live outside you, and not crush you from inside."

Ellie nodded, finding her voice again. "Simone's right. Even if no one reads them now, they'll exist. They'll matter."

Claudette looked between the two of them, her smile rueful but tender. "You both sound like Norma," she said again. "So, let's see what she sent me." She opened the envelope and unfolded a letter slowly. Her eyes scanned the sheet and she laughed.

Ellie raised an eyebrow at Quinn.

"You know," Claudette said, holding up a USB stick with a grin, "your Aunt Norma loved to create things. She is a genius with technology and I can only imagine what she's created here."

"Aunt Norma? *My* Aunt Norma is a tech genius?" Ellie asked.

Claudette placed the USB stick on the table beside her. "Oh, my, yes." She nodded. "We have a video chat every week. When the ability to do this first came out, Norma wrote me and said we had to try it. She'd learned all about it on the internet and had bought herself a new computer. That's when she started talking about you and your group. My granddaughter had just set me up with a lovely laptop and I am now convinced writing my story is a good idea."

Claudette let out a sigh and Ellie realized she must be tiring.

"Why have I never heard about you, yet you seem to know so much about me?" Ellie sat back, only to shift as the velvet buttons on the old chair dug into her shoulder.

"Everyone has secrets, my dear, even your aunt."

"We know she worked on codes at the end of the war," Ellie offered.

Claudette nodded. "Ah, she finally told someone. Good. Here, let me read this to you."

My Dearest Claudette,

As I sit down to write this letter, I can almost hear the scratching of your pen on paper across the sea. Seventy years of ink and paper, of folded secrets and shared joys, what a life we've lived together through words.

From the very first letter, when we were both just girls trying to understand a world torn by war, I knew there was something extraordinary about you. Your grace, your fire, your beautiful way of seeing the world; those things reached me across an ocean and never left.

Though we never met in person, your friendship has been one of the truest constants of my life. You have walked with me through every heartache and every celebration, always from afar, yet never feeling far at all. You taught me the soul doesn't need proximity to be close.

There is so much I wish I could give you in person: a hug, a cup of tea, a shared afternoon by the window. But since life had other plans for our meeting, I'm sending a piece of my heart instead. Something I hope will remind you of all the love we've carried together for nearly a lifetime.

Ellie is delivering this because I could not bear for it to be lost or handled without care. It is for your hands only, dear friend. Please know what you find inside is not just a gift, but a testament to seventy years of laughter, tears, dreams, and letters. Our letters.

One day, perhaps in another place, we'll sit face-to-face. Until then, I remain—

Forever your friend,

Norma

Claudette grasped the USB stick, her eyes wet. "She's put all the letters I sent her on here! Everything we experienced and shared. I'm sure I've forgotten half of them, but this will be delightful."

The light had changed by the time Ellie glanced toward the tall windows. A quick check of her watch revealed that it was after lunch. She could hear Quinn's stomach growling. She stood with reluctance, Quinn following. "We should let you get back to your designs, Madame Claudette. And Simone, thank you for the tea. It was lovely."

Claudette waved a plump hand dismissively. "You will call me Claudette. 'Madame' makes me sound like a teacher about to scold you. And you..." her eyes twinkled as she looked at Quinn, "...you will come again, scar and all. It suits you, you know."

Quinn inclined his head with a trace of a smile. "Not everyone agrees, but I'll take the compliment."

Simone rose, moving with that same feline grace she had shown at the door, though now her composure carried warmth instead of hauteur. She crossed to a small writing desk, tore a sheet from a notepad, and scribbled something quickly. Folding it once, she handed it to Ellie.

"My number. For when the group meets," she said. Then, with a flicker of hesitation, she added, "And for anything else."

Ellie tucked the note carefully into her bag, and quickly dashed off her phone number before handing it to Simone. "Thank you. I'll make sure Aunt Norma knows you're both officially enlisted."

"Bullied," Claudette corrected as she came to stand by her granddaughter's side, but her eyes were shining.

Ellie laughed. "Bullied with love, then."

They all moved toward the door together. Simone opened it, but not before leaning down to kiss her grandmother's cheek. The gesture was tender, unguarded, and Ellie found herself smiling at the sight.

"Au revoir, Ellie. Quinn." Claudette's voice was warm, almost motherly. "You go with my blessing, and my thanks. Tell Norma she has not lost her touch."

"We will," Ellie promised.

Out in the corridor, the air felt cooler, quieter, as though the apartment had been its own world; bright, vivid, brimming with stories waiting to be told. Ellie glanced once over her shoulder, catching a final glimpse of Claudette framed in the doorway, Simone beside her, the two generations so different yet bound together.

As the door closed gently behind them, Quinn let out a low whistle. "Your aunt certainly keeps interesting friends."

"She does. And I think they're about to become *our* friends, too."

Together, they stepped out into the bright Paris afternoon, carrying with them the promise of new stories yet to be written.

Chapter Six

Ellie adjusted the strap of her small leather crossbody bag and pulled her scarf a little tighter around her neck. The afternoon Paris sun was lovely, but she felt a slight chill in the air. Beside her, Quinn glanced down at the city map he had taken from his bag and was now folded awkwardly in his hands.

"You realize," Ellie teased, "every person in the city can spot us as tourists from a mile away with that giant map?"

Quinn smirked. "It's called *being prepared*. Besides, my phone is at forty-three percent. I don't want to risk depending on Google Maps."

"Forty-three percent? The drama." She rolled her eyes playfully. "Fine, fearless navigator. Lead the way."

Claudette's apartment was near the Opéra Garnier, and they were intent on seeing as much of Paris on foot as possible. The city, Ellie insisted, had to be walked, its charm revealed itself slowly, block by block.

They began down Avenue de l'Opera, the grand façades gleaming in the mid-day light. Shops were open, and the aroma of butter and pastry floated from cafés as bakers carried trays of croissants to the front counters.

Ellie stopped suddenly in front of a patisserie. "It's way past lunch and I heard your stomach growling in Claudette's apartment." Behind the glass sat golden croissants, pain au chocolat with shiny, dark seams of chocolate, and delicate fruit tarts arranged like jewels.

Quinn raised an eyebrow. "Do you think they're as good as Maggie's?"

"It's Paris," Ellie replied simply, pushing the door open. They emerged five minutes later, each with a flaky croissant wrapped in a square of white paper.

"This is so decadent for lunch," he murmured, his mouth full and his eyes closing in pleasure.

They ate as they walked, brushing crumbs from their clothes. The buttery pastry practically melted on the tongue. Quinn sighed. "All other croissants are canceled. This is the standard now."

"We can't tell Maggie," Ellie said, holding out her pinky finger. Quinn grasped it with his pinky and they shook on the promise.

They wound their way south, weaving through smaller streets until the wide expanse of the Seine opened before them. The river glimmered silver under the sun. Bookstalls lined the embankment, their green boxes propped open with vintage posters, old French novels, and watercolor sketches.

Ellie leaned over a wooden stall, fingers skimming a stack of postcards. "These are gorgeous. Imagine sending one home with the Eiffel Tower sketched in watercolor. It feels so... cinematic."

Quinn flipped through an assortment of black-and-white photographs. "Half of these look like they were taken in the fifties. You can practically hear the accordion music."

After buying a few of each, they walked through Square de la Tour Saint-Jacques until Notre-Dame came into full view. Despite some scaffolding still wrapping sections of the cathedral, its rose windows and iconic towers loomed majestically. They crossed the bridge and slowed as they came to the front of the building.

Ellie grew quiet, taking it in. "It feels unreal to stand here. Like history is still humming through the stones."

Quinn pointed out the gargoyles jutting from the sides. "They look like they're judging us."

"Maybe they're wondering how many more centuries of tourists they'll have to endure."

They circled the cathedral slowly, agreeing to return for a more thorough visit.

They crossed the Pont au Double, pausing halfway to watch tour boats glide beneath them. The breeze carried laughter and snippets of multiple languages.

"How are your feet holding out?" Ellie asked, as she leaned against the bridge's side and stretched out one foot, then the other.

"Not bad," he answered, though he didn't mind the rest.

The narrow streets of the Latin Quarter spilled them into a different mood entirely; bohemian, lively, with tiny bookstores squeezed between cafés. At Shakespeare and Company, Ellie insisted they go inside.

Rows upon rows of English-language books filled the cramped rooms. Quinn perched on a stool by the poetry shelf while Ellie hunted for a French cookbook with English translations.

"You're telling me," Quinn said, "you want to lug a giant cookbook around Paris all day?"

Ellie grinned. "Yes, but think about cooking from it back home. A souvenir that feeds us."

They compromised on a slim paperback, as they both knew that Ellie's dreams of being a chef were just that, dreams. The cashier stamped it with the shop's famous logo. Ellie held it like a treasure.

They headed north again, following the Seine and crossing the Pont Neuf. Ellie stopped every few steps to take photos; the dome of the Institut de France, the glitter of the river, the endless stream of Parisian traffic, somehow more elegant than chaotic.

Soon the Louvre spread before them. The glass pyramid gleamed in the sunlight, surrounded by the palace's sweeping wings. Tourists clustered everywhere, snapping selfies.

Quinn tilted his head. "Do we go in?"

Ellie hesitated. "The line looks brutal. Besides, we'd lose the whole day inside. Maybe tomorrow?"

"Tomorrow, then." Quinn took a dramatic bow. "The Mona Lisa will have to wait."

They lingered in the courtyard, marveling at the scale, then followed the Jardin des Tuileries east. Children sailed toy boats across fountains, and chairs were scattered around for lounging. Ellie pulled Quinn toward one.

"Sit. Pretend we're Parisian intellectuals pondering art and philosophy."

Quinn leaned back with exaggerated seriousness. "I think, therefore, I am... hungry again."

They found a small brasserie near Place de la Concorde. Nothing fancy, just simple café tables outside, facing the street. Ellie ordered a croque monsieur, Quinn a quiche Lorraine. They shared a bottle of sparkling water, the carbonation tickling their throats.

"This is the life," Ellie said between bites. "Café chair, city buzzing, zero responsibilities."

Quinn nodded. "We should establish a rule. Every time we travel, at least one day must be entirely wandering on foot with no schedule."

"I second that motion."

The sun grew warmer as they finished eating, then strolled up the Champs-Élysées. Shops gleamed with polished windows, luxury brands mingling with familiar chains. Street performers entertained tourists, juggling or strumming guitars.

Ellie paused outside Ladurée, mesmerized by the rows of pastel macaroons in the window. "We'll come back later," she promised herself aloud.

The avenue carried them straight to the Arc de Triomphe, massive and solemn in its position at the traffic circle. They craned their necks to take in the carvings and the eternal flame beneath.

"Want to climb it?" Quinn asked.

Ellie winced. "Hundreds of steps after walking all day? Let's admire from below this time."

"Agreed. My legs are already sending complaint letters to management."

They wandered west along Avenue Kléber until the unmistakable lattice of the Eiffel Tower rose above the trees. Ellie gasped. "There it is. The cliché of clichés. And yet... I'm in love."

Quinn grinned. "It looks like it belongs on every postcard for a reason. And tomorrow afternoon, we go to the top." He felt Ellie's arm twitch next to him. She hated heights.

They walked past the grand structure and Ellie craned her neck to see the top. That was higher than she might be comfortable with. They continued on and entered the Champ de Mars, weaving through crowds sprawled on the grass. Street vendors approached with miniature tower keychains jingling. Ellie declined politely, then tugged Quinn toward a bench.

They sat in companionable silence, watching as the sun dipped lower. The iron tower shifted from silver-gray to warm bronze in the changing light.

Ellie rested her head briefly on Quinn's shoulder. "This is the kind of memory that sticks."

Their legs ached and their feet protested every step, so they took a taxi back to their hotel. Inside their room, Ellie collapsed onto the bed with a groan. "We walked half of Paris."

Quinn dropped the map on the desk. "My phone's at twelve percent. Tragedy averted."

They stretched out on their bed for a twenty-minute nap then took energy rejuvenating hot showers. They changed into evening clothes; Ellie in a simple black dress with a deep red silk scarf, Quinn in a crisp button-down and jacket.

"Ready for dinner?" Quinn asked, offering his arm.

"Beyond ready."

***

Quinn had reserved a table at Le Meurice, the Michelin-starred restaurant inside a historic hotel overlooking the Tuileries. From the moment they stepped into the gilded dining room, Ellie felt transported. Crystal chandeliers glimmered overhead, frescoes decorated the ceiling, and tables gleamed with white linens.

A maître d' guided them to a table near the windows. Ellie whispered, "I feel like we should whisper. This is so elegant."

Quinn glanced around. "If I accidentally knock over a fork, I might be escorted out."

Their waiter approached with menus, describing each course with reverence. Ellie's eyes widened at the poetic descriptions, lobster with citrus emulsion, pigeon roasted in its jus, desserts that sounded like art installations.

They chose the tasting menu, though without wine pairings. Instead, they requested sparkling water and fresh juice.

A rise in voices caught their attention and they looked to the entrance to see a man enter the room followed by two larger men. The maître d' showed them a table at the side, surrounded by empty tables and calm.

The young man looked around and nodded at a few people who were staring open mouthed at him and his group.

Ellie also had her mouth open.

"You'll catch flies like that," Quinn murmured and grinned as she snapped her jaws shut.

"Is that?" She raised her hand to point then snapped it back into her lap.

Quinn nodded. "Lewis Hamilton." He was as much in awe as his Formula 1 mad new wife, but he managed to glance Lewis's way with more finesse.

"There's no race in France," she whispered, fighting with herself to stop looking at her hero.

"They are on a weeks break," Quinn reminded her, "and he has the right to eat wherever he wants."

"Well, he has good taste," she said just as their amuse-bouche arrived. Ellie redirected her attention and closed her eyes after the first bite. "This is dangerous. If the tiny pre-meal snack tastes like this, how am I supposed to survive the rest?"

Quinn nodded solemnly. "We may not make it."

Two more small dishes arrived and they left nothing on their plates. The main course was roasted pigeon with foie gras and truffle jus. Ellie hesitated for a moment, but after the first bite she murmured, "Okay, this is extraordinary. Rich, but delicate somehow."

Quinn agreed. "I didn't even know pigeon could taste like this. Back home, they're just city birds."

For dessert, they were presented with a sculptural masterpiece: a sphere of white chocolate that melted when warm raspberry coulis was poured over it, revealing layers of mousse and sponge inside.

Ellie gasped. "It's like performance art. And edible!" Her comments were louder than she had intended and she quickly looked around to find Lewis smiling at her as his table stood up to leave. He winked. She grinned, but felt a red wave of heat creep up her neck. It was made even worse when she caught Quinn's eye. How awkward to have a crush at her age.

"He's a snappy dresser too," Quinn said, returning the nod Lewis sent his way.

She took one last look at her favorite driver then sighed. "You didn't plan that, did you? Because I'm never sure what's fate and what's not with you."

"*We* are fate, and so was that," he took her hand and kissed her knuckles.

They finished the meal with tiny bite sized macaroons, madeleines, and dark chocolate truffles. "I have to tell Maggie about this," Ellie said. "Do you think it would be rude to take pictures?" She started to pull her phone out of her purse, but slid it back when she saw Quinn's raised eyebrow. "Yes, of course it would be."

They took their time, lingered and enjoyed the ambiance of the restaurant. Conversation was light and comfortable. Quinn's hand reached across the table and their fingers stayed entwined as they finished every morsel in front of them.

By the time they stepped out of the restaurant, the city glittered under lamplight. The Louvre pyramid glowed faintly in the distance. Their feet dragged, their stomachs full, their hearts light.

Quinn stretched. "I don't think I've ever eaten like that in my life."

"Same," Ellie said, looping her arm through his. "I also don't think I've ever walked this much in a single day. My body is both blissful and destroyed."

They reached the hotel, changed into their pajamas, and flopped into bed.

Ellie yawned. "Tomorrow, we'll conquer more. But tonight... we're done."

Quinn clicked off the lamp. "Best early night ever."

Within minutes, the city hummed beyond their window while they drifted into deep, contented sleep.

Chapter Seven

While Ellie and Quinn started their walking tour of Paris that day, back in Percyville, the early morning light slanted through the square window of Virginia's tiny house, catching the dust motes as they floated lazily in the air. A half-packed box sat open on the butcher-block countertop, its flaps sagging outward as if tired of being filled. Virginia knelt beside another box on the floor, carefully wrapping a porcelain teacup in layers of newspaper. Even though she had lived here for a short time, the house already had a stripped-down feeling, her life peeled back gently, one possession at a time.

The place was small, hardly more than two hundred square feet, but there was a sweetness in its arrangement. Every corner bore the marks of care: the slender wooden staircase rising to a loft tucked beneath the peaked roofline, the narrow bedroom on the main floor, the tiny iron stove set into a stone hearth in the sitting area, the walls paneled with pale pine. It was tidy, minimal, but not cold.

Phil knocked and surprised her out of her memories. "Come in," she called.

He ducked under the doorway beam as he entered, pulling the tape measure from his jacket pocket. He froze, eyebrows raised. "I forget how space feels different in a tiny house. Looks small on the outside, but it surprises you inside."

Virginia smiled, tucking a strand of silver hair behind her ear. "It's like a seashell. You don't expect it to have so many curves inside. You'll get used to it. Norma is coming over to help with my final bits and pieces, after you all meet with Graham."

Phil nodded. "I can't believe we have a new mystery to solve so soon. But it's just what we all need." He clicked out the tape measure with a metallic snap, then knelt by the wall beneath the loft ladder and measured. "This is perfect for my bookcase, if I trim the crown molding." He wrote the measurement in a little notebook he carried, then scrambled sideways to measure the next stretch of wall.

Virginia leaned on the counter, watching him. His shoulders were hunched, and his hair a brilliant white; his movements cautious and careful. She loved that she could give him this, and felt a warmth seeing him here, fussing over measurements as if the act itself were a small claim to belonging.

"You'll make it yours in no time," she said softly.

Phil glanced up at her, tape measure still extended. "That's the plan." He gave a faint smile, but there was heaviness in it.

Virginia noticed, but she didn't press. Instead, she reached for another mug from the cupboard, one of the few she hadn't boxed yet. "Coffee?"

"Always."

While the coffee pot gurgled on the tiny two-burner stove, they worked in companionable silence. Phil stretched the tape across the narrow living room, muttering numbers under his breath, while Virginia folded cardboard flaps over her keepsakes.

When the coffee was poured, thick and black in mismatched mugs, they sat at the little table tucked under the window. Outside, the woods pressed close around the house, autumn leaves fluttering in the breeze.

Phil sipped, then set his mug down, staring at the grain of the table. "You ever think about how quickly time goes?" he asked suddenly.

Virginia raised her brows. "Every day."

He chuckled, but it came out low, almost bitter. "It sneaks up on you. One day you're chasing kids around, the next... you're measuring walls in a house half their size."

Virginia tilted her head. "You sound like you're grieving something."

Phil hesitated, then looked away toward the tiny fireplace. The firebox was empty now, the stove cold. "I haven't seen my son in... what, three years now? Feels longer."

Virginia stayed quiet, letting the words settle between them.

Phil rubbed his jaw. "We had a falling out. I won't go into details; it's not the kind of thing you air out. But it was bad enough he cut me off. Holidays come and go, birthdays... nothing. I send him messages, but they just vanish into the void."

Virginia reached across the table and put her hand on his. His fingers were rough, callused, but they trembled slightly under her touch. "I'm sorry, Phil."

He swallowed. "I keep wondering what I'll leave behind when I'm gone. If my kids will even know who I was. My daughter; she's good to me. Lives out west in Vancouver. She visits when she can. She's over the moon about me moving here. Says the grandkids think it's like a treehouse."

Virginia's face softened into a smile. "That's beautiful."

"Yeah," Phil said, but his eyes were clouded. "But then I think about my son. About the gap. Whole pieces of family history might never get passed on to his kids. And even my daughter, I worry. What do they really know about me? About where we come from?"

Virginia took a sip of coffee, then leaned back. "But now that you're into genealogy and writing your own memoir, do you still feel the same?"

Phil blinked. "To be honest, it's still a jumble at times. There's so much to go through."

"Yes. Like remembering stories, finding photographs, deciphering old letters. I've been at it for years. My father started it, really. He had this box of papers, land deeds, marriage licenses, yellowed photos. When he passed, I was given the box. And now I spend hours in archives, tracing back names. I've got records going back to the 1700s. Sometimes I think it's the most important gift I can leave: the story of where we came from."

Phil tilted his head, intrigued despite his heaviness. "I really should make more of an effort to get things together. I've got scraps of papers, documents, and tons of photographs."

"Ellie says begin with yourself," Virginia said simply. "You write *your* story. The rest branches out from there."

Phil chuckled softly. "My story's messy."

"Messy is still history," she said. "Your grandchildren won't want perfection, they'll want truth. They'll want to know who you were, the good, the struggles, the lessons."

Phil was quiet for a moment, listening to the click of the coffee pot cooling on the stove. Then he said, "Sometimes I think my son hates me so much he wouldn't want to know any of it."

Virginia shook her head gently. "We can't predict the future. Wounds close in unexpected ways. Even if he doesn't want it now, one day he might. Don't deprive him of the chance to know you, even if you never see him again. A written history, which is your voice on paper, could be a bridge. A quiet one, waiting."

Phil's throat tightened, and he looked down at his mug. They sat in silence, the weight of memory between them. Finally, Phil exhaled, long and slow. "I like that. A bridge."

Virginia smiled. "I'll show you some of my binders before I pack them away. Maybe it'll spark ideas."

Phil nodded, his face softening.

Virginia lit a small fire in the stove, its crackle filling the little house with warmth. Flames danced, throwing orange light on the stacked boxes.

Phil crouched by the hearth, holding his hands near the glow. "I'll admit, this little stove sold me on the place. Feels like an anchor. A fire always makes a home feel alive."

Virginia settled into the armchair opposite. "That's why I loved the main floor bedroom. People think tiny houses are just lofts, but I needed a space where I could sit by the fire and still feel rooted."

Phil turned, looking around with new eyes. The loft above was now empty, the floor around them held boxes, sealed and neatly stacked, waiting for Virginia's family to come and take them away. The ladder rungs gleamed from years of use. On the shelf near the window sat a single framed photo: Virginia's parents, long gone but still watching.

"You've made this place a story in itself," he said.

Virginia nodded. "But now it's your turn. You'll bring your furniture, your books, your pictures. You'll add chapters."

Phil smiled faintly, then grew thoughtful again. "Do you ever think about what's lost? The stories no one wrote down?"

"All the time," Virginia admitted. "That's why I started writing my own memories. And why this group drew me so fast. The way my grandmother baked bread, the way my uncle told ghost stories by lantern light. The details fade if we don't catch them."

Phil rubbed his chin. "I remember my father teaching me to fish. The smell of the riverbank, the way he showed me to tie the line just so. Haven't thought about that in years. My daughter doesn't know those stories. My son definitely doesn't."

"Then write it down," Virginia urged. "Even if no one reads it today, someday someone will open a box, find your words, and it will be like hearing your voice again."

Phil's eyes shone with quiet resolve. "Maybe that's what I need to do. Not for me, but for them."

Virginia leaned forward, her voice warm. "Exactly. We're all temporary stewards of memory. Passing it along is the best legacy we can give."

Phil nodded, staring into the fire. The crackling flames lit the lines of his face, softened them, made him look almost boyish for a moment. "Well, that's it then." He stood and patted his pocket to make sure his notebook was secure. "I've got my measurements, and I know some of the furniture will never fit in here."

"Toss what you don't need anymore." Virginia walked him to the front door, all three steps away. "I've enjoyed meeting you, Phil, meeting everyone and sharing this trip down memory lane. And I'm glad you're taking over the Nest."

Phil raised an eyebrow.

"That's what I call her." She patted the doorframe. "You can name her anything you'd like."

"Why change a good thing?" He held out a hand, then let out a whoosh as Virginia pulled him close for a hug.

"Now off you go," she pushed him out the door. "Graham has a mystery to solve, and tell Norma she can stop by any time."

Phil hurried down the Tiny House Haven road, past a couple of other homes, and up Graham's walkway to the porch. The sky was darkening and he could feel rain coming. He turned to see Virginia watching from her door and sent her a jaunty wave, which she returned with an added thumbs up.

***

Phil walked into Graham's tiny house to find him and Norma sitting at the counter. This house had no separate dining table but the space between his friends was ample enough to have spread out the documentation Graham had about his grandfather and Lucien Tremblay.

"All done?" Norma asked Phil as he pulled an extra stool from underneath and placed his laptop in the only empty space in front of him.

He patted his pocket and notebook. "All done but the moving. I'll have to make some hard decisions about what to bring with me and what to pass on or toss, but I've pretty much made up my mind on that. Oh, and Virginia says come whenever you can, there's no rush."

Norma sighed. "I can't believe she's leaving so soon. She just got here." She shook her head, annoyed with the whine that had crept into her voice. "But I know she'll be happier with her family. All she talked about were those grandkids of hers."

"Come to think of it," Phil said, head tilted as he regarded her with slit eyes, "I've never heard you talk about your grandchildren."

Norma heaved another sigh. "That's because there's only one, and she lives out west. And I'm not a traveler, and my son is very busy."

Graham and Phil exchange a glance.

"But I do get to see her through video chats, so that's good." Norma added with a bright smile that didn't quite reach her eyes. She pointed at the documents. "So, where do we start?"

The hint was taken, and the subject changed.

"I think the first thing to do is find out if my grandfather was actually in Baie-Saint-Paul around 1892-1893."

"Census return of 1891 is the closest census that might give us that information," Norma said.

Phil booted up his computer.

"Can I get you something to drink?" Graham offered, half rising from his seat, only to drop back down when both Norma and Phil shook their heads.

"What location or county are we looking for?" Phil asked once the Ancestry site was open. "What jurisdiction was Baie-Saint-Paul under?"

Norma grabbed her phone and typed in quickly. "Charlevoix."

Phil typed that in, then looked up at Graham. "And your grandfather's name was Stuart Brody, right?"

Graham nodded. "Yes. And he was born in Scotland."

Phil's fingers tapped out the information and hit enter. "Here we go. He's living as a boarder in the home of Francois Girard and his family.

Mr. Girard is a medecin, and Stuart is also listed as a medecin under occupation."

"That would be what they called a physician in French," Norma said.

"His birthplace is Scotland, as was that of both his parents," Phil continued reading the entry. "He was single at this time, was Presbyterian, and aged twenty-six."

Graham sat back, one hand on the table, the other adjusting his glasses nervously. "We found him. I honestly didn't believe we would, or that any of this was true."

"Why not?" Norma asked. "Or did you hope it *wasn't* true?"

Graham shrugged. "Maybe that."

"I'm going to screen shot this and save a copy as well so you can take your time with it later," Phil said.

"Ellie taught you well, Padawan," Norma joked. The Star Wars reference went over both the men's heads. Norma shook hers and rolled her eyes.

The rain tapped harder against the tiny house windows as the three huddled in the cozy warmth. The small stove in the corner ticked as it cooled, and a faint smell of maple still lingered from the morning's fire.

"Alright," Graham said, cracking his knuckles with exaggerated ceremony. "Time to go Tremblay family hunting."

Norma laughed. "You make it sound like we're setting off into the woods with rifles."

"Well," Phil said, tugging his sweater tighter around his chest, "in a way, we are. The woods just happen to be... digitized." He gestured to the glowing Ancestry homepage on the screen.

Graham leaned forward, his eyes bright. "Okay. We know we're looking for my father's half-brother, Lucien Tremblay. But let's find Lucien's mother, Émilie. She's the thread, right? She ties him back to the Tremblays of Charlevoix."

Norma nodded. "If we can find her in the 1891 census, we'll know where she was, and maybe who her parents were."

Phil's fingers flew across the keyboard, entering the search: *Émilie Tremblay, 1891, Charlevoix, Quebec.* The screen blinked, loading. The three of them leaned in, the glow illuminating their faces like a campfire.

"There!" Graham jabbed the screen. "Émilie Tremblay. Age twenty. Living with..." He squinted to read the names. "François Tremblay and Marie. Her parents."

"Got them!" Norma grinned. "That's one piece of the puzzle. What's their address?"

Graham frowned. "Huh. Doesn't say. Just lists the district, subdistrict, and enumeration page."

Phil leaned back, folding his arms. "That's how it was back then. No addresses. Just... 'this farm, that concession.'"

"Which is frustrating," Norma muttered. "We can't exactly put 'Concession No. 3, Charlevoix' into Google Maps."

Phil clicked through the digitized images of the census page. Lines of looping handwriting scrolled past. Beside Émilie's name was the neat number "20," her age, and next to her father's name, the word *cultivateur*. Farmer.

"That makes sense in this region," Graham murmured, leaning over to see the screen.

"So, if we don't have an address here, maybe we leap forward," Phil suggested. "The 1901 census. Schedule 2 sometimes listed street addresses, right?"

"Exactly," Norma said. "Or at least more detailed locations. Let's see if they're still there ten years later."

Phil typed again, pulling up the 1901 census. The search results took longer to load, and for a moment the only sound in the room was the patter of rain. Finally, the page resolved.

"There they are," Graham whispered. "François Tremblay, Marie, Lucien, aged eight. But no Émilie. Does it give an address?" Graham leaned in again.

"Not exactly. Just says Baie-Saint-Paul. But..." Phil scrolled further. "Schedule 2 should have more detail. It sometimes lists concessions and lot numbers."

They clicked through to the scanned images, grainy but legible with patience. The column headers stretched across the page: *Street, avenue, road, name of building or lot*. Graham's eyes darted down the lines.

"There," Norma said suddenly. She pointed to a faint entry. "Concession rang... I think it says Rang Saint-Laurent. That's a road!"

Graham's eyes widened. "So that's where their farm was. Rang Saint-Laurent, Baie-Saint-Paul."

Phil whistled low. "That's a real place. We could find it on a modern map. It might not be the exact house, but... we'd be walking the same road."

The three of them stared at the screen, imagining it: a dirt road curling along the hillside, wooden barns with sagging roofs, fields opening onto the St. Lawrence River in the distance.

"Okay," Graham said at last, snapping out of the reverie. "Now let's check the 1911 census. See if Émilie is there."

Norma sighed, stealing a quick look at Graham. "I think we can assume from her letters she was quite ill, and probably died in between the census returns."

Phil pulled up the 1911 census. "It's still just the three of them. No Emilie. Lucien is now eighteen."

"And the 1921 census?" Norma asked, shifting forward on her seat.

Phil typed in Lucien's information and the results came up almost instantly this time.

"Yes!" Graham said. "There he is. Lucien Tremblay. Head of household, age twenty-eight. Married. Wife, Elise. And look! A son. René. Two years old."

Norma clapped her hands. "You found them! That's your ancestor right there, with his little boy."

Phil squinted at the list of household members. "But where are François and Marie? The grandparents. They should be here, shouldn't they? Unless..."

"Unless they died," Norma said softly. "We should double-check."

Phil quickly typed in François Tremblay and Marie in the 1921 census. The screen came up empty. He tried again with variations of spelling, Tremblai, Trembley, even Trombley. Nothing.

"They're gone," Graham said finally, his voice quieter. "They must have died sometime between 1901 and 1921. They'd have been pretty old by then."

Norma nodded. "At least we know they didn't just move away. If they're not showing up anywhere in Charlevoix, and they're not in Quebec City... it's safe to say they passed."

The rain had thinned to a drizzle when Graham spoke again. "Okay. If they're not in 1921, we should check parish records. Their deaths were probably registered in Baie-Saint-Paul."

Norma scooted her chair even closer. "Good idea. Ancestry sometimes has the Quebec parish registers scanned. Let's try '*François Tremblay, Baie-Saint-Paul, death between 1901 and 1921.*'"

Phil typed, the keys clattering in the silence. The results loaded slowly, as if the system were reluctant to give up its secrets. Then, there it was.

"François Tremblay," Graham read aloud. "Died 1915. Age seventy-eight. Listed as farmer. Cause of death not recorded, but burial at Église de Baie-Saint-Paul."

"Wow," Norma whispered. "There it is. His final record."

Graham leaned over, tapping the screen. "And if he died in 1915, Marie might not be far behind. Try her next."

"Wait, his death record also lists his wife's maiden name," Phil said, squinting at the screen. "Give me a second." He searched again. A few false hits, too young, wrong parish. Then, the right one appeared. "Marie

Gagnon, veuve de François Tremblay," he said softly. "Died 1917. Age seventy-four. Same parish. Buried in the cemetery of Baie-Saint-Paul."

For a moment, none of them spoke. The silence of the tiny house was filled only by the continued tapping of rain on the window.

"It's strange," Graham murmured, "seeing the dates like that. François in 1915, Marie in 1917. They were right there on the farm in 1911, and then... gone before Lucien was even raising his own family."

Norma touched his arm gently. "But you found them. You know where they are now."

Phil sat back, his expression thoughtful. "And we know exactly where to look. The parish churchyard. They'll be there, side by side."

"Can we look for Emilie's death as well?" Norma asked quietly. "We need to finish her story."

When Phil brought up Emilie's parish burial record, Norma gasped. "She died when Lucien was only five years old. Can you imagine that poor boy growing up without a mother?"

"He had his grandparents," Phil reminded her. "And probably a dozen aunts, uncles and cousins."

"If not more," Graham said. "But that's a family tree for another day."

The three of them sat in silence for a moment. The rain had eased, and now only a dripping sound came from the eaves outside. The stove ticked again, almost like a clock.

"You know," Phil said at last, "this is incredible. You've got three generations right there on census records. The grandparents in 1891, the mother in 1901, and Lucien himself in 1911 and 1921. That's a straight line."

"And a place," Norma added. "Baie-Saint-Paul. Rang Saint-Laurent. We can trace them not just in time, but in space."

Graham leaned back, exhaling slowly. "I can almost picture it. Lucien as a little boy, running through the fields, helping his grandfather with chores. Then, twenty years later, still on the same land, but now with his own wife and child." He rubbed his eyes, blinking away the strange weight in his chest. "It makes them feel real. Not just names on a tree."

Phil pushed his chair back slightly, stretching. He looked from the glowing laptop screen to Graham's thoughtful face. "You know what?"

"What?" Graham asked.

"We should go there."

"Go where?"

"To Baie-Saint-Paul," Phil said, a spark in his voice. "Why not? It's not that far. We could walk those roads ourselves. See the land they farmed, maybe even find the church where they're buried. The census gave us the map, but the place itself..." He spread his hands. "The place will tell us the rest."

Norma's eyes lit up. "I love that idea. Field trip! We could visit the archives, maybe talk to the parish priest. They'll have baptismal and burial records. And photographs, maybe."

Graham felt a grin tugging at his lips. The idea was almost overwhelming, but it stirred something deep inside him. "To Baie-Saint-Paul," he said quietly. "Where the Tremblays lived, worked, loved... and are buried."

Phil raised his arm as if holding a sword. "To Baie-Saint-Paul."

Norma laid her hand upon his. "To the Tremblays."

Graham lifted his hand and covered Norma's. "To finding them."

The rain started hard again outside, steady and rhythmic, as though echoing the pulse of history calling them forward.

Chapter Eight

Ellie pressed her hand against the smooth brass rail as she and Quinn mounted the last of the stone steps into the Musée Carnavalet the next morning. The air outside still carried the smell of fresh baguettes from the boulangerie down the street, but inside the museum it was cooler, hushed, and weighted with centuries.

Plans had changed. "I know we should visit the Louvre, and see the Mona Lisa, but I think the Musee Carnavalet will be more interesting. For both of us."

"I enjoy art, but not the crowds the Louvre will have," Quinn admitted. "And learning history never hurt anyone." He tucked his sunglasses into his collar and whispered. "Smells like old paper and polished wood."

Ellie smiled, her eyes wide as though she'd just entered a cathedral. "That's exactly what I wanted. History should smell like this."

She'd found this museum mentioned on social media that morning. The Carnavalet, she had learned, was the museum of Paris itself; a labyrinth of rooms and galleries dedicated to the city's memory, from medieval walls to the Revolution to the art deco salons. She hoped somewhere within she might catch a glimpse of the world her ancestor might have known.

They passed through the opening atrium, tiled in black-and-white marble, where a grand staircase spiraled upwards. The walls bore plaques engraved with the names of Parisian neighborhoods, each letter chiseled as if they were saints in a litany.

Ellie stopped in front of a large model of the island of Paris, Notre Dame Cathedral towering over the buildings below. "Oh, Quinn, look." She stood on tiptoe, then walked all around it. "This was his Paris."

Quinn leaned in beside her. "It looks like a maze."

"It was crowded, uneven, twisting. The city wasn't like the neat boulevards we see now. That's later—Haussmann's Paris, 19th century. In 1600, Paris was medieval still. Narrow lanes, open sewers, wooden houses leaning so close the rooftops nearly touched."

Quinn whistled softly. "So, your ancestor made shoes in a city that smelled... worse than the Métro in July."

Ellie laughed, covering her mouth. "Much worse. Imagine mud, horse dung, and tanneries all together. I don't know if he came to Paris, or stayed in his small town. But still, this was the Paris of Henry IV and Louis XIII. A place of guilds and apprenticeships. Shoemakers were organized in confréries—brotherhoods. They had rules, rituals, even patron saints."

Her tone carried reverence. She looked again at the streets, as though her relative might appear any moment, hurrying with a bundle of leather beneath his arm.

They moved on into a room lined with portraits; bourgeois families in stiff collars and somber blacks. Glass cases displayed guild charters, their Latin text illuminated with curling flourishes.

Ellie stopped before a parchment where a pair of shoes had been drawn in the margin, an emblem of the shoemakers' guild.

"Here it is," she breathed. "The Compagnons Cordonniers."

Quinn tilted his head. "Compagnons... like companions?"

"Exactly. But in France it meant journeymen; craftsmen who traveled from town to town, working, learning, proving themselves before becoming masters. Shoemaking was essential, of course. Everyone needed shoes, from peasants to nobles. But it was also regulated. You couldn't just open a shop. You had to train, to swear loyalty to the guild, to respect its statutes."

She leaned closer, reading aloud the list of rules posted beside the parchment: "*No master may take more than two apprentices. No shoemaker may sell outside the market without permission. No false leather is to be used upon pain of fine.*"

Quinn smirked. "So basically, even then, there were quality-control issues."

"Yes!" Ellie's eyes lit. "Shoes were life. Roads were filthy, streets uneven. Good shoes meant protection, health, status. A noble's boots might be embroidered in silk, while a laborer's clogs were wood and leather. Every sole told a story." She gazed at the parchment as though it were a relic, her ancestor's invisible hand hovering above it.

The next gallery opened into reconstructed rooms: a merchant's kitchen with copper pans, a bourgeois salon with tapestries, and, Ellie's favorite, a tiny shoemaker's workshop.

She gasped when she saw it. A wooden bench scarred with knife marks. Awls and needles laid in a row. Strips of leather hung like drying laundry. Wooden lasts, forms shaped like feet, stood waiting.

Quinn bent to examine a half-finished shoe. "Looks uncomfortable. Pointy toes, stiff leather. Not something I'd wear to go for a long walk in."

Ellie shook her head. "That was the style. And leather softens with wear. Imagine sitting here all day, hands stained with dye, the smell of tallow candles and boiled glue everywhere. My ancestor might have spent his whole life in a room like this."

She longed to touch the edge of the bench, but was careful not to cross the barrier rope. Her voice grew quieter. "This... is closer than any photograph. It's like stepping into his world."

Quinn watched her, noting how her usual brisk energy had slowed, softened. She was usually the one dragging him from exhibit to exhibit, reciting dates and facts with professor-like certainty. But here, in this shoemaker's corner, she looked almost vulnerable, as though something fragile and immense had opened inside her.

“Hey,” he said gently, “if he could see you here, tracing his life back four centuries, I think he’d be proud.”

She laughed shakily. “Or confused. He’d probably say, ‘Why is my great-great-great-granddaughter staring at my workbench like it’s a shrine?’”

Quinn grinned. “Well, you do have a tendency to worship history.”

“Guilty.”

They sat for a moment on a bench near the window, sunlight spilling across the parquet floor.

Ellie opened the small notebook she carried everywhere. “Paris in the 1600s,” she murmured, jotting notes. “Population nearly half a million. The largest city in Europe after London. Political tension between Catholics and Protestants. Henry IV was assassinated in 1610, Louis XIII still a child. Streets narrow, overcrowded. Epidemics frequent. Yet also art, theater, music flourishing. The Hôtel de Ville rebuilt, Place des Vosges constructed.”

Quinn leaned back, letting her voice paint the city. “So, your ancestor walked through streets alive with both danger and brilliance. Plague on one corner, poetry on the next.”

“*If* he was here, yes. And shoemakers were everywhere; at markets on the Pont Neuf, near the Île de la Cité, in the Marais. They made boots for soldiers, slippers for courtiers, sturdy work-shoes for artisans. Some specialized in patins, which were overshoes with wooden soles to lift people above the mud.”

Quinn raised his eyebrows. “So, they basically invented platform shoes.”

Ellie giggled. “In a way. Except more practical. Fashion and necessity have always tangled.”

She scribbled another note. “I want to know if he was a master with his own shop in his home town, or just a journeyman. Did he wander around France with his trade or...” She glanced at him and sighed. “I have so many questions, and most will never be answered.”

Quinn reached over and squeezed her hand. "I'm sure you'll find some answers. You're tenacious like that."

They continued through galleries filled with carved shop signs; giant painted boots, wooden gloves, copper kettles, symbols once hung above Parisian storefronts.

"Look," Ellie said, pointing to a sign shaped like a golden shoe. "That would have told passersby what the shop sold. Most people couldn't read, so signs were pictures."

Quinn tilted his head. "Like proto-logos."

"Yes! Branding before branding. Imagine the pride of hanging that above your doorway."

***

At noon they stepped into the museum's courtyard café. Ivy trailed across stone walls, pigeons cooed from ledges, and the scent of espresso mingled with fresh croissants.

Ellie stirred her coffee slowly. "The 1600s were a turning point. Paris was shifting from medieval chaos to baroque grandeur. The shoemakers' world must have felt both traditional and changing."

Quinn bit into his egg sandwich. "Kind of like us visiting here. We're tourists with smartphones, but still craving connection to something ancient."

Ellie smiled. "Maybe that's human nature. We always want to stand in both worlds at once." They finished eating in silence, people watching, enjoying the ambiance. "I came here hoping to learn facts; dates, guilds, practices. But what I really feel is... atmosphere. Texture. Smell. The feeling of a city alive with both filth and beauty, where every pair of shoes mattered."

Quinn nodded. "I'm glad we came here. It was very enlightening."

She smiled. “I can almost imagine him, sitting in his shop, stitching leather by candlelight, never guessing that centuries later someone would stand in a museum and whisper his name.”

Quinn paid the bill, and they headed out of the museum. He slipped his arm around her. “Are you ready for the Eiffel Tower?”

Ellie groaned but smiled at him. “What time is our reservation?”

Quinn pulled out his phone and checked. “Four o’clock. We’ll take the elevator all the way, stopping on the second floor to change and have a look around.”

“Then we’ve got time to go back to the hotel for a rest?” Ellie raised an eyebrow. “I admit, I’m tired. Between all the walking and the time change, I’m not a spring chicken anymore.”

“Oh, thank goodness,” he raised an arm and hailed a cab, ushering her into the back seat and flopping beside her with a grin. “A nap would be amazing.”

***

They left their shoes by the door and headed straight to the bed. Each issued a tiny groan as they let their limbs stretch out. Eyes closed.

Ellie’s phone buzzed on the end table beside her. She looked at the caller.

“Tell them to go away,” Quinn whispered.

“It’s my Aunt Gillian,” Ellie said, sitting up as she read the text. “I sent her a message from the plane the other day that we were coming to France for our honeymoon.” Ellie looked at him. “She wants to have lunch with us while we’re here.”

“She’d come all the way to Paris just to have lunch with us?”

Ellie shrugged. “Apparently. Would you mind? I mean, it *is* our honeymoon and...”

Quinn waved a hand in the air. "Wouldn't mind at all. I like Gillian. She's interesting."

Ellie's finger was poised above her phone. "When would be a good time?"

"When we get back from Rivièreclaire," Quinn muttered, his eyes closing.

"When is that?" Ellie asked.

"Two days from now," he whispered before his face went slack and his breaths came out even in the fashion of someone deep in sleep.

Ellie typed furiously, waited for a confirmation response, then put her phone away. She snuggled back down on the bed, careful not to disturb Quinn, but close enough to feel his heat.

With a deep sigh, she drifted off to the muffled sounds of Paris outside their window.

Chapter Nine

Quinn was looking forward to this. When they crossed the Champ de Mars and finally stood in the shadow of the Eiffel Tower, Ellie craned her neck until her scarf slipped loose around her shoulders. The iron latticework rose impossibly high, carving its dark silhouette against the late afternoon sky. It was both delicate and enormous, like lace forged from steel.

"Pictures never do it justice," Ellie murmured.

Quinn smiled at her awe. "Ready to go up?"

Her expression tightened. "About that..."

He raised his eyebrows knowingly. "The famous Ellie vs. Heights saga?"

Ellie folded her arms. "I never said I wouldn't do it. Just that I might... freak out halfway."

"Then I'll be your emotional support human." Quinn produced his phone from his jacket pocket and wiggled it. "Too late to back out now. Tickets are bought and waiting."

They joined the queue, the murmur of a dozen languages swirling around them. Vendors drifted by, their keychains jingling and miniature towers gleaming in the fading sunlight. The air smelled faintly of roasted chestnuts from a nearby cart.

When they reached the entrance, Quinn scanned his QR code and the attendant gestured them forward. Ellie's pulse quickened.

The glass-and-metal elevator waited like a cage attached to steel rails. As soon as the doors opened, a surge of tourists flooded out, some with wide grins, others slightly green. Ellie hesitated, then stepped inside, flattening herself against Quinn's side.

The ascent began with a shudder. The floor trembled under their feet as the city slipped away. Through the large windows, beams of wrought iron crisscrossed in dizzying patterns. Beyond them, rooftops dropped lower and lower.

Ellie squeezed Quinn's hand hard enough to make him wince. "Talk to me. Distract me. Anything."

He didn't miss a beat. "Okay, rapid-fire questions. Best French pastry?"

"Croissant."

"Wrong. It's pain au chocolat. Favorite landmark so far?"

"Notre-Dame."

"Wrong again. It's clearly the Arc de Triomphe because it looks like a massive stone donut."

Despite herself, Ellie let out a nervous laugh. "That's ridiculous."

"Ridiculously accurate."

The elevator slowed, and the doors opened with a hiss. They had reached the second level.

A cool gust of wind swept over them as they stepped out. The platform was crowded but spacious, with railings lining the perimeter. The grated floor let slivers of daylight peek through, revealing the terrifying drop below. Ellie froze.

"Nope. Nope, nope, nope. That's a trap. Floors this high in the air should *not* have holes."

Quinn gently steered her toward the inner section, away from the edge. "We don't have to go close yet. Just... walk with me."

Together, they circled the level. Even with the stores and restaurants available, the view tugged at Ellie's eyes despite her fear. The Seine shimmered like a ribbon of light, boats cutting trails through the water. The golden dome of Les Invalides gleamed in the distance. Farther still, Sacré-Cœur perched on Montmartre like a white crown.

Tourists pressed against the railing, phones raised high. A couple kissed dramatically with the city behind them. Children ran circles around their parents, squealing.

Quinn coaxed Ellie a little closer. “Just one quick peek. I’ve got you.”

Her stomach lurched, but she forced herself forward. Fingers white-knuckled around the railing, she dared a glance.

And it was… breathtaking.

The city unfurled in perfect geometry; tree-lined boulevards radiating outward, pale stone buildings stacked like toy blocks, bridges spanning the river in elegant arcs.

“Oh,” she whispered, her fear momentarily forgotten. “It’s beautiful.”

“Told you,” Quinn said softly.

For a moment, they stood together in silence, the wind brushing their faces, Paris sprawling infinite below them. Quinn took a quick selfie; catching Ellie with her windswept hair and a half grin, and himself thankful to be with her, with Paris stretching out beyond them.

A lot of people stopped at the second level, but Quinn tilted his head toward the next set of elevators. “Want to go higher?”

Ellie’s eyes widened. “Higher? Isn’t this enough?”

“Come on. The top is supposed to be magic.”

She bit her lip, torn between dread and determination. “In for a centime, in for a euro,” she muttered finally.

The elevator to the summit was smaller and more crowded. And each wall was pure glass. As it ascended, the beams of the tower fell away, leaving only sky and horizon. Ellie shut her eyes tight, her nails digging into Quinn’s hand.

“Distract me again,” she whispered fiercely.

Quinn thought quickly. “Okay, you’re designing the ultimate picnic basket. What’s in it?”

She groaned. “Really?”

“Yes. Go.”

"Fine. A baguette, obviously. Cheese. Grapes. Maybe macarons for dessert."

"Wrong," Quinn said cheerfully. "The correct answer is: two baguettes, three kinds of cheese, and at least six macarons, because you always need backup."

The elevator jolted to a stop. When the doors opened, Ellie blinked in disbelief.

They had stepped into open sky. The summit platform was narrower, the wind sharper. Paris stretched in every direction, horizon melting into hazy blue.

Ellie clung to Quinn's arm but let him guide her in a slow circle. Landmarks dotted the cityscape like a map come alive.

"There's Montmartre, with Sacré-Cœur," Quinn pointed. "And over there, La Défense; see the cluster of skyscrapers? Completely different vibe."

Ellie's voice was hushed. "It feels like the whole world is down there. Like I'm floating above it."

"You're conquering Paris right now," Quinn said with mock solemnity.

She gave a nervous laugh. "More like surviving it."

They paused near a coin-operated telescope. Quinn dug in his pocket for a coin, slid it in, and gestured for Ellie to look.

She hesitated, then bent cautiously. Through the lens, the Arc de Triomphe sprang into sharp focus, tiny cars swirling around it like ants. She gasped. "That's insane."

Quinn leaned close. "You're doing it. See? Not so bad."

"Don't push it," she muttered, but her cheeks were flushed with exhilaration.

Eventually, the wind grew colder and the crowd denser. They made their way back to the elevator, descending first to the second level, then down toward the ground.

This time, Ellie kept her eyes open. Watching the city rise up to meet them, she felt a strange relief, and a flicker of pride. When they stepped off the final elevator and her shoes hit solid pavement, she exhaled dramatically and spread her arms.

"Thank you, earth," she declared. "I will never take you for granted again."

Tourists around them chuckled. Quinn shook his head, laughing. "You're ridiculous."

Ellie shot him a grin. "But I did it."

"Yeah, you did." He slung an arm around her shoulders as they walked away. "Next time, we'll skip it?"

"Definitely," Ellie said. Then, after a pause: "Or maybe not. Ask me in ten years."

They turned back once more. The tower loomed above them, both terrifying and magnificent. Ellie felt the knot of fear in her chest loosen into something else, something like awe. She was surprised to find the sky turning lavender, the last streaks of daylight draining into deep blue. They had stayed longer than she thought. Spotlights blinked on, illuminating the Eiffel Tower from base to summit. The iron lattice glowed golden, impossibly bright against the darkening sky.

Ellie stopped in her tracks. "Okay, I thought it was impressive before, but now? It's like a lantern for the whole city."

Quinn tilted his head back. "I read somewhere that Parisians hated it when it was first built. Called it ugly."

Ellie scoffed. "They were wrong. This is..."

The tower burst into a thousand sparkling lights, glittering in a five-minute spectacle. Gasps rippled through the crowd. Children squealed. Couples clutched each other, phones raised to capture the magic.

Ellie's jaw dropped. "Oh my goodness."

Quinn laughed softly at her expression. "Better than fireworks, huh?"

She couldn't tear her eyes away. "It's like... it's alive." When the sparkle faded, applause scattered among the onlookers. Ellie finally blinked, cheeks flushed. "Okay, you win. Totally worth facing my fear."

Quinn pulled her close and kissed her gently. "I love you, wife of mine. Your courage is admirable."

As they wandered away from the tower, the scent of something sweet and warm drifted through the cool night air. Ellie's nose twitched. "Do you smell that?"

They followed the aroma to a small crêpe stand tucked along the sidewalk. A man in a flat cap worked quickly over a hot griddle, spreading batter thin and golden before filling it with Nutella, sugar, or fruit.

Ellie pressed her hands together like a prayer. "Yes. A thousand times yes."

They ordered two: one Nutella-banana for Ellie, straight fruit for Quinn. The vendor folded them into cones of paper, the edges steaming in the night air.

Ellie took a careful bite, chocolate smearing the corner of her mouth. Her eyes closed in bliss. "Okay, this is officially the best food in Paris."

Quinn raised his brow. "Better than the Michelin-star pigeon?"

She pointed at him with her crêpe. "Don't make me choose. Different categories of greatness."

They leaned against a low stone wall overlooking the Seine, eating in silence for a few minutes while the city sparkled around them. Boats glided by, their decks lit with strings of bulbs. Music floated faintly over the water.

Quinn nudged Ellie with his shoulder. "This is better than any souvenir."

She nodded, her mouth full. "Agreed."

They set off along the river, the pavement glowing under lamplight. The Seine reflected everything, the lights of bridges, the shimmer of passing cars, even the twinkling tower far behind them.

Ellie looped her arm through Quinn's. Her legs ached from the day's walking, but she didn't care. The rhythm of their footsteps, the low murmur of other strollers, the distant sound of an accordion, it all wove together into something dreamlike.

They paused at Pont Alexandre III. The bridge gleamed with gilded statues, its lamps ornate and glowing like jewels. Ellie sighed. "Every corner of this city looks staged for a movie."

They continued past Les Invalides, its golden dome shining against the dark sky. The streets grew quieter as they neared their hotel.

By the time they reached the lobby, Ellie could barely lift her feet. "I don't think I've ever been this tired and this happy at the same time."

Quinn hit the elevator button. "You conquered the Eiffel Tower, ate the world's best crêpe, and walked half of Paris. That's a solid day."

Ellie leaned against his shoulder as the elevator doors closed. "Tomorrow, remind me I'm supposed to be on my honeymoon. I might just stay in bed until noon."

"Except that we have an early train in the morning," Quinn reminded her. "Family awaits."

In their room, Ellie kicked off her shoes and collapsed onto the bed. Quinn loosened his jacket, draped it over a chair, then joined her, echoes of their afternoon nap.

She yawned. "That definitely takes precedence," she agreed before dragging herself up to head to the bathroom. Ten minutes later she was back, waiting for Quinn to return from his shower.

Through the cracked window, the distant hum of traffic, laughter from a late-night café, and the occasional wail of a siren drifted in.

Ellie rolled onto her side on the bed, eyes already heavy. "Quinn?"

"Yeah?"

"Thanks for holding my hand. Literally. Up there."

He brushed her hair back gently. "Always."

She smiled, half-asleep. "Good. Because I'm never going up a tower again without you."

Within minutes, she was asleep, the glow of the city faint on her face. Quinn lay beside her, listening to the quiet rhythm of her breathing, and thought maybe, just maybe, Paris had given them its best kind of night: exhausting, dazzling, unforgettable.

Chapter Ten

The highway stretched northeast, the St. Lawrence River shimmering on their right in patches through breaks in the forest. The early morning sun slanted across the dashboard, glinting off Graham's glasses as he leaned slightly forward, both hands steady at ten and two.

"Feels good to be on the road again," he said, though his knuckles were white. "It's been years since I drove this far in one go. My knees may not forgive me."

From the passenger seat, Norma, neat in her pressed cotton blouse and with her always-present notebook perched on her lap, gave him a sidelong glance. "If your knees give out, Graham, you've got two capable co-pilots here. Well, one capable and one stubborn." She tilted her head toward the back seat.

Phil snorted. "Capable? I'll have you know I've been driving since before you had your first high heels. And unlike some people, I don't need a map glued to my lap."

Norma's pen tapped the page. "I prefer the term 'prepared,' thank you. At least when I'm navigating, we don't end up in Vermont by accident."

"Ah, that was only once," Phil said, his laugh filling the car like a brass instrument. "And my kids loved it."

Graham smiled but kept his eyes on the road. "All right, children, let's not rehash the detours of past adventures. Today's mission is Baie-Saint-Paul, and what we might find out about the Tremblay family."

They all grew quiet. The car hummed steadily over the asphalt. Beyond the windshield, the land rose and dipped, with farmhouses scattered like little squares of white and red across the fields. They had left at the crack of dawn to beat rush hour traffic, and Maggie had supplied muffins and coffee. Getting through Montreal had been easier than expected, and now they were eating up the miles, passing cars heading the other direction, into the city for another day of work.

Norma broke the silence. "Did you know that Charlevoix County is named after French Jesuit explorer Pierre Francois-Xavier de Charlevoix after his travels in the area? And some of the parish registers go back to the late 1700s. A genealogist's dream."

Phil groaned. "A dream for you, maybe. For me, it's a headache in Old French cursive I can't read without a magnifying glass. If then."

"That's why I'm here," she said brightly. "My eyesight's still sharp. And besides, the stories buried in those registers, baptisms, marriages, burials, they're not just names. They're whole lives."

"Whole lives reduced to one line in a book," Phil muttered. But his voice softened. "Still, it means something to you, Graham. So, it means something to us too."

Graham's throat tightened. He blinked at the horizon, letting the hum of the tires fill the space before answering. "I just want to know more about Lucien. My father never spoke much about his side of the family, and I would have remembered if he mentioned having a half-brother. If Baie-Saint-Paul is where my grandfather worked for a while, and where Lucien was born, I need to see it. To stand where they stood."

Phil leaned forward between the seats and patted his shoulder. "We'll get you there, buddy. One way or another."

***

They stopped at a rest area to trade places. Phil insisted on taking the wheel for the middle part of the journey, stretching his arms dramatically before climbing into the driver's seat. "Step aside, Captain," he announced. "The ship now has a proper pilot."

Norma rolled her eyes but settled comfortably in the back with her notebook. Graham eased into the passenger side, rubbing his knees. As they pulled back onto the road, the conversation shifted.

"So," Phil said, squinting at the ribbon of highway ahead, "any of you ever heard of the Great Meteor of Charlevoix?"

Graham chuckled. "You mean the impact crater? I read about that last night as I was looking into the history of the area. It shaped the whole region. The mountains around Baie-Saint-Paul aren't just hills; they're the rim of a meteor strike from hundreds of millions of years ago."

"See?" Phil wagged a finger. "I knew there was something cosmic about this trip. You're not just chasing your roots, Graham, you're heading straight into a crater. A family crater."

"More like a cosmic cradle," Norma corrected. "The geography shaped settlement patterns, the soil, the rivers. Families grew where land could feed them. You can't separate history from the land."

Phil grinned. "And here I was hoping for UFOs."

"You watch too many late-night documentaries," Graham said.

"Better than all those genealogy webinar links Norma sends us," Phil shot back.

"You enjoyed the one about old ship passenger lists," she reminded him.

"Only because the presenter had a Scottish accent. Made me feel like I was in an episode of a detective show."

Norma chuckled and turned a page in her notebook. "Well, you'll have plenty of accents in Charlevoix. The French spoken there has its own flavor, like old words preserved, a bit different from Montreal French. Don't embarrass us by asking for 'poutine' the wrong way."

Phil gasped theatrically. "How dare you assume I'd mis-order fries, gravy, and cheese curds. I'm practically bilingual in comfort food."

The kilometers passed, conversation drifting between serious and silly. Norma read aloud a list she'd printed: "Baie-Saint-Paul parish registers begin in 1681. The early families include Tremblay, Bouchard, Simard, and Gagnon. Do any sound familiar, Graham?"

"Obviously the Tremblay, now," Graham said after a pause. "Isn't Tremblay like Smith in Quebec, everywhere?"

"True," Norma agreed. "But connections matter. A cousin here, a godparent there, it adds up. We'll have to comb carefully."

Phil interrupted, "Speaking of combing carefully, do either of you know what that smell is?" He sniffed the air dramatically. "Please tell me it's cow pasture and not my thermos leaking in the back seat again."

Norma cracked the window. A gust of country air rushed in, carrying hay and manure. "Pasture," she confirmed, hastily closing the window. "Though if Maggie packed us egg salad sandwiches, I'm not vouching for the ride home."

They all laughed, the kind of laughter only good friends can share, loose and forgiving.

***

By mid-morning, the landscape grew hillier. Forests thickened, pines rising against a deepening blue sky. The St. Lawrence came into view again, wide and shining.

Graham leaned toward the window. "There it is. That's the river they followed. Imagine it filled with canoes, wooden boats, families clinging to hope, trying to start anew along these banks." His voice was hushed, reverent.

Norma set her notebook aside, simply looking with him. Even Phil's usual commentary faded for a moment.

Finally, Phil said quietly, "I suppose every family story starts with someone daring to take that first step. Or paddle."

"Exactly," Graham said. "And now, here we are, following their trail."

They stopped for a muffin break at a rest stop near Montmorency Falls. Norma handed out the food and divided up the semi- hot coffee into plastic cups.

"I've been to these falls before," Phil said before taking a bite of Maggie's muffin.

"Are they as amazing as I've heard?" Norma asked.

Phil nodded. "They are indeed. I have a few more to mark off on my bucket list of Quebec falls, but Montmorency is a highlight."

"Maybe we'll see them on our next visit," Graham said, crumpling his muffin wrapper up and handing it to Norma to put in the bag.

"You're sure we'll be heading on more adventures?" Norma asked.

"One never knows," Graham answered.

With snacks finished, they switched drivers, this time Norma took the wheel. She adjusted the seat forward with practiced efficiency. "You two behave," she said as she merged onto the highway. "I don't need backseat drivers."

Phil leaned back with a grin. "You're in charge, General."

The conversation meandered again, as it usually did with them: childhood memories, television shows they half-remembered, and now the added delight of both men moving into tiny homes.

At one point, Norma asked, "What's the earliest ancestor each of you actually knows about?"

Phil scratched his chin. "My great-grandfather. Farmer in Ontario. All I know is he had a moustache that could sweep a barn floor. The photo still hangs in my cousin's hallway."

Graham smiled faintly. "I guess for me it's my great-grandfather, Colin Brody. I'm still not sure of the truth of all the stories I've heard about him, but I fully intend to find out."

"And me?" Norma said thoughtfully. "My mother's line is better documented, Nova Scotia Acadians. But what interests me is how stories survive. My grandmother used to tell us how her family hid in the woods during the deportation. It was called the Great Upheaval. They eventually came to Quebec to settle. Whether it's true or not, it anchored us."

Phil whistled. "That's heavy. I've just got moustache man."

"Every family's got its flavor," she said.

***

The sun was high in the sky when road signs began pointing toward Baie-Saint-Paul. The town nestled between mountains, its church spire already visible in the valley below.

"Almost there," Graham whispered from the back seat, wiping his palms on his pants.

Phil noticed and reached forward, turning down the radio that had been playing golden oldies for the last half hour. "Hey, don't go having a heart attack on us now."

Norma slowed the car around the last bend. The view opened: the St. Lawrence gleaming, the town laid out along the riverbank, white steeple rising proud. "There it is," she said softly.

Graham swallowed hard. "There it is."

The car descended into Baie-Saint-Paul, the streets lined with old stone houses, galleries, and shops. Flower boxes spilled red geraniums, and signs in French swung gently in the mid-day breeze.

As they drove slowly through the town, Graham felt a strange warmth in his chest, a mix of belonging and awe.

Phil turned to him. “Well, Graham, looks like your ancestors had pretty good taste. Not a bad place to start a dynasty.”

Graham laughed shakily. “No, not bad at all.”

Norma pulled the car into the inn’s parking lot and turned off the engine. Silence settled, broken only by the ticking of the cooling motor. They sat a moment, none of them rushing to open the doors.

Finally, Graham said, “Tomorrow, we go to the archives. Now, we breathe.”

“Agreed,” Phil said, stretching. “And maybe find a decent lunch. Preferably something without egg salad.”

Norma smiled, tucking her notebook into her bag. “And after lunch, maybe a walk about.”

They climbed out of the car, stiff but content, three seniors on a quest. Ahead lay records and mysteries, but for now, the air smelled of woodsmoke and river water.

And for Graham, that was enough.

Chapter Eleven

The early September sun lay over the valley like a soft shawl, gilding the river and painting the rooftops of Baie-Saint-Paul in shades of copper. The town was picture perfect, nestled between rolling green hills, with tidy houses, colorful shutters, church spires, and the faint scent of pine from the surrounding countryside.

Norma, her silver hair catching the light like spun glass, glanced up at the building they would stay in for the next couple of nights. "It's beautiful, Graham. Look at those flower boxes. She must take such care."

Phil gave a low whistle. "This is exactly what I imagined when you said 'B&B in Quebec'. Old wood, a porch with rocking chairs, and probably the smell of fresh bread waiting inside."

They stood before a three-story house with pale yellow siding and a wraparound veranda. Climbing vines clung to the railing, dotted with late-summer blossoms, and the front door was painted a cheerful teal.

Graham took a deep breath. "Ready?" he asked, his voice both eager and cautious.

Norma looped her arm through his. "Ready. Though I think I'm mostly ready for a cup of tea."

Phil grinned. "And maybe pie. Don't forget pie."

Together, they mounted the porch steps.

The door opened before Graham could touch the handle. A woman of about sixty, brisk but smiling, stepped out, wiping her hands on a striped apron. Her dark hair, streaked with gray, was pulled back into a bun, and her hazel eyes sparkled with welcome.

"Bonjour, bonjour! You must be Mr. Brody and company," she said, her accent a lilting blend of French and English. "I'm Madeleine, the proprietor here. Bienvenue!"

"Thank you," Graham said, holding out his hand. "Yes, Graham Brody. These are my good friends, Norma and Phil."

She shook each hand warmly, then ushered them inside. The entry smelled of citrus polish and baking bread. Phil's nose rose in the air to take a deep whiff and a smile crossed his face. Norma nudged him and grinned.

To the left, a sitting room opened, with overstuffed armchairs facing a stone fireplace. Quilts in muted reds and blues hung neatly folded over the backs of chairs, and a grandfather clock ticked companionably in the corner.

Norma sighed contentedly. "Oh, it feels like we've stepped into someone's home rather than a hotel."

"That is the idea," Madeleine said, clearly pleased. "Here we are family, not just guests. I like to think of it that way. Now, let's get you settled before you tell me your plans."

"I don't mean to be rude," Phil said as he picked up his bag, "but are you from here? I ask because your English is impeccable, yet I hear an accent."

"My husband was English," she said. "I taught him French and he taught me English. And our children are Franglais."

At Graham's frown, Norma leaned in and said, "That means they speak French with a lot of English."

Madeleine led them up a narrow staircase. The walls were hung with framed black-and-white photographs of the Charlevoix region, depicting farmers in wide fields, children in Sunday clothes before a church, a ferry crossing the St. Lawrence. Graham slowed once or twice, drawn to faces that might, just might, carry some echo of the man he sought.

Madeleine opened the first door with a flourish. "This will be for you, Mr. Brody. It is our best room. We call it the Aubépine."

Inside was a bright chamber with a tall four-poster bed, white coverlet embroidered with tiny blossoms, and lace curtains that framed a view of the rolling hills beyond. A writing desk stood in the corner; its surface polished to a soft sheen.

Graham set his bag down. "This will do nicely."

Phil poked his head in. "Nicely? Graham, this is like stepping into a heritage magazine. I bet you'll start writing letters with a quill at that desk."

They all laughed.

The next two rooms were equally inviting: Norma's was pale blue, with a quilted bedspread and shelves of books in French and English; Phil's was tucked beneath the eaves, cozy and cheerful, with a small dormer window looking down onto the garden. Once they'd glanced around, they regrouped in the hall.

"Now," Madeleine said, clasping her hands, "before I forget, we settle the accounts at the beginning. It is easier that way. Two nights for the three rooms, breakfast included. Is that all right?"

"Yes, of course," Graham said immediately, reaching for his wallet.

Phil opened his mouth, but Graham silenced him with a look. "This is my project, my family's search. I told you I was covering this."

Norma touched his arm. "Thank you, Graham. That's very generous."

He shrugged, almost embarrassed, and handed over his card. Madeleine slipped it through a small machine she fetched from downstairs, humming softly as she worked.

"There we are. All set."

As she handed back his card, Madeleine asked, "So, what brings you to Baie-Saint-Paul? Tourism, hiking, the art galleries?"

Graham hesitated, then decided there was no point in delay. "Family, actually. I'm looking for information about someone who lived here, my half-uncle, Lucien Tremblay."

Madeleine's eyebrows rose. "Tremblay is a very old name here, very common. But Lucien ... ah, that is more specific."

Norma leaned forward eagerly. "He would have been born around 1893. We don't know much more. Graham only recently discovered the connection."

Phil added, "We're hoping to trace records; maybe parish books, land deeds, anything."

Madeleine pursed her lips thoughtfully. Then her face brightened. "You should speak with Denise Grégoire at the archives. She is an expert on local families. If anyone knows about a Lucien Tremblay, it will be her."

"The archives?" Graham repeated, almost reverently.

"Yes. It's not far, just down the hill, housed in the old convent. Denise is usually there in the afternoons. I suggest you go today, while the sun is still bright."

Graham felt a flutter of anticipation. "Thank you, Madeleine. That's ... exactly what we needed."

Norma reached across and squeezed his hand. "See? Already doors opening."

Madeleine waved a hand. "But before research, you need food. Always. There is a little restaurant I send all my guests to, Le P'tit Chou, only a few minutes' walk from here. Very charming, with soupe aux pois, tourtière, fresh bread. You will like it. They also do a hearty supper."

Phil groaned happily. "Tourtière? I'm in."

"Go," Madeleine urged, "enjoy yourselves. Then you will have the strength to face dusty registers and old handwriting."

They stepped back into the sunlight, following Madeleine's directions down cobbled lanes lined with galleries and bakeries. Window boxes spilled over with geraniums; a church bell chimed in the distance. The town bustled quietly, locals greeting one another in French, tourists pausing to snap photos.

Norma inhaled deeply. "I love how the air smells different here."

Phil slowed, taking it in. "And the colors. Look at those roofs, every shade from green to bright red. It's like the whole town is showing off."

Graham walked between them, feeling oddly grounded. He couldn't believe in a matter of days the whole story of his family had changed. Now here he was, standing in the place where Lucien had once walked, perhaps had laughed, worked, lived.

***

The restaurant was exactly as Madeleine promised: a small café with wooden tables, sun streaming through lace-curtained windows, and a chalkboard menu in neat cursive. A cheerful woman in her thirties greeted them with "Bonjour! Hi!" and ushered them to a corner table.

Phil leaned back, sighing. "If we don't find Lucien, at least we'll find good food."

They ordered: soupe aux pois and crusty bread to start, and tourtière for the main course for all of them. When the food arrived, steaming and fragrant, conversation softened into appreciative murmurs.

Outside, Baie-Saint-Paul's main street was quiet except for the occasional rattle of a delivery truck, but inside the three friends sat at their corner table, their coats draped over the backs of their chairs.

Norma tore off a piece and buttered it slowly. "It feels strange, doesn't it? Being here, knowing Lucien grew up in this very town."

Graham blew on his spoon, then nodded. "Strange, yes. But exciting too. If we find him, it'll be like opening a door I never knew existed."

Phil grinned and leaned back. "And if we don't, at least we've had a good excuse to eat like kings. This soup is worth the trip alone."

Norma chuckled. "You and your stomach. But it will be amazing to add to your family tree, Graham."

Graham nodded. "I do love a good mystery, and trying to stitch the missing parts of the family together before they vanish is fascinating."

Phil dipped his bread into his soup and looked thoughtful. "See, that's the difference between us. You're writing to connect the dots backward. I'm writing to clear the clutter in my head before I move into the tiny house. Sort of like packing only what matters, but with memories instead of furniture."

Norma smiled, watching the steam rise from her bowl. "And I'm writing because I don't want my grandkids to think I was just a voice on the phone at holidays. I want them to know how stubborn I was, and how many times I changed my mind before finding some kind of peace."

The waitress returned with plates of tourtière, the crust golden and flaky. She set them down with a practiced smile and disappeared again. The three sat for a moment, taking in the sight and smell before cutting into the pies.

Phil spoke around a mouthful. "Funny thing about the tiny homes, people think it's about shrinking your life. But for me, it's the opposite. It's about making space for stories, not stuff. If I only have a hundred square feet, then my memories have to live bigger than my walls."

Graham tapped his fork against his plate. "That's beautiful, Phil. Though I'm not so poetic. I just want to make sure Lucien's name isn't forgotten. Even if my writing is more like a ledger than a poem, it's something real."

Norma reached over and patted his hand. "And that's the point, isn't it? Each of us leaving behind a trail, in our own way. Yours may be a ledger, Phil's a confession, mine a collection of stubborn lessons, but together, they make a map."

Outside, a church bell tolled one o'clock. The three of them lifted their glasses of water and clinked them gently, the sound small but sure in the cozy restaurant.

"Here's to Lucien," Norma said softly.

"And to stories," Graham added.

Phil raised his glass higher. "And to living small, so our words can live large."

After their plates were cleared, the waitress brought small cups of strong coffee and a shared slice of sugar pie, its sweetness rich against the bitter coffee. They lingered over it, reluctant to break the spell.

Through the window, the sun spilled over cobblestones, and the murmur of French voices floated in like music.

Norma leaned back with a sigh. "This town ... it feels like it holds its history close, doesn't it? Like the past is just under the surface."

Graham nodded. "Which makes me hopeful. Somewhere in these streets, Lucien left traces. Baptism, school, maybe a marriage record."

Phil grinned. "Maybe even a scandal. Every family has at least one."

Norma shook her head in mock reproach. "Phil!"

But Graham only chuckled. "If there is, we'll find it. For better or worse." Finally, he pushed back his chair. "Shall we? Madeleine said afternoons are best for finding Denise at the archives."

They rose, paid, and stepped back into the brightness of the day. The path toward the archives wound past art galleries spilling canvases onto sidewalks, each one depicting the river or mountains with vivid strokes. The scent of baking still clung to them, but now there was something sharper in Graham's chest: anticipation, like a door opening onto an undiscovered room of his own life.

Norma slipped her hand into his, and Phil, walking a step ahead, turned with a grin.

"Well, friends. Let's go meet this Denise Grégoire and see what she can tell us about the man who's been waiting all this time for us to come looking."

And together, they walked toward the convent building that housed the archives, sunlight gilding the path before them.

Chapter Twelve

The convent rose above the town like a guardian: long gray stone walls, tall arched windows, and a bell tower that caught the afternoon light. Its grounds were edged with lilac bushes and maples whispering in the warm breeze. The three travelers paused before its heavy wooden doors, suddenly hushed by the sense of time they carried.

Graham stared upward. "Imagine how many people have walked through here, carrying their stories."

Norma touched the sleeve of his jacket. "And now we add ours."

Graham pushed open the door. "Let's find Denise before I lose my nerve."

Inside, cool stone greeted them. The entryway was wide, with vaulted ceilings and polished floors that echoed underfoot. A small sign directed them toward the archives, and soon they found themselves in a large reading room lined with shelves and filing cabinets.

Behind a desk stacked with folders sat a woman in her fifties with short dark hair, glasses perched on the bridge of her nose, and a red scarf looped around her neck. She looked up as they approached, her eyes sharp but kind.

"Bonjour. You are visitors, yes?"

"Yes," Graham said quickly, stepping forward. "My name is Graham Brody. Madeleine from the B&B sent us. She said you might be able to help."

At the mention of Madeleine, the woman's expression warmed. "Ah, of course. I am Denise Grégoire. Please, sit." She held out a hand and handshakes were exchanged all around.

They lowered themselves onto wooden chairs before her desk. Denise folded her hands. "Now tell me what you seek."

Graham cleared his throat, suddenly aware of the weight of his request. "I am looking for information about someone who lived here, a man named Lucien Tremblay. He would have been born around 1893. I only recently discovered he was my father's half-brother."

Denise tilted her head, thoughtful. "Tremblay is one of the oldest names in Charlevoix. But Lucien ... I think I may recall something. Let us see." She rose with a swish of her scarf and moved to a tall cabinet, sliding open a drawer filled with index cards. Her fingers danced lightly across them.

Graham leaned forward, every nerve taut.

At last, she plucked a card and read silently, her lips moving. Then she glanced up. "Yes. Lucien Tremblay. Born here in Baie-Saint-Paul, in 1893. His mother was Émilie Tremblay."

Graham's breath caught. "Yes, that's them!"

Denise returned to the desk, setting the card before them. Her handwriting was neat, the letters precise. "I can bring you the baptism record. That will give you both his parents' names, date of birth, the godparents."

She disappeared again, this time into a back room, and returned with a large, leather-bound register. Its pages were yellowed, edges fragile.

Norma frowned. "How is it you have the original register here?"

"It was common for the parish priest to make a copy for government authorities, and keep one here," Denise told her. "Our parish has asked that we keep their original documents in this building. It's been renovated and is a better environment for them." She searched the register and opened it to a page, turning the book so they could see.

"There," she said softly, pointing to an entry in French script.

Graham bent close, eyes tracing the faded ink. *Lucien Tremblay, né le 14 février 1893. Parents: Émilie Tremblay.*

Norma whispered, “No father noted.”

Phil squinted. “But *she* knew who the father was!”

Graham nodded slowly. “She must have had some reason not to disclose it. But that would have made her life quite difficult, being a single mother.”

Denise listened intently. “It was more common than you think.”

“We found her death record online; she died in 1898,” Phil said.

Denise flipped through a few more pages and stopped. “Here. This must be what you saw. Émilie died in 1898. She was only twenty-eight years old.”

Norma clasped her hands. “That’s the one. Which means Lucien was just five.”

Graham felt a hollow ache open in his chest. He stared at the elegant black script that reduced a young woman’s life to a line in a ledger. “So he lost his mother almost before he knew her.”

Denise nodded solemnly. “After her death, the child might have been raised by family. That, too, was common then, especially if the father could not or would not raise him.”

Phil frowned. “We know he was raised by his grandparents, and we believe his father never even knew about him.”

“He obviously didn’t,” Graham said softly. “He came back to New Brunswick and started the family I grew up knowing. And Lucien was left here.”

Denise seemed to consider something, then rose again. “Wait a minute. I believe I have seen his name in another source recently.”

She disappeared into the back, the sound of her footsteps echoing faintly. The three sat in silence.

Norma reached for Graham’s hand, squeezing it. “It’s not your fault,” she murmured. “You couldn’t have known.”

“I know,” Graham whispered. “But to think of him ... five years old, suddenly without his mother ...”

Phil said gently, "Maybe those grandparents loved him deeply. Maybe he had joy here."

At that moment, Denise returned, carrying a folder. She slid out a clipping from a newspaper, carefully placing it on the desk. "This is from Le Charlevoix, 1902. A small article about the Tremblay farm."

They bent over it. The headline read: *Jeune garçon vit avec ses grands-parents à la ferme familiale. Cette année, il a remporté le prix de la plus grosse citrouille.*

"It says here," Denise translated, "that young Lucien lives with his grandparents on the family farm, and that this year he won the prize for the biggest pumpkin."

Norma's eyes misted. "So he did stay with them. He wasn't left adrift."

Phil pointed suddenly. "Look at that! There's even a photograph."

Indeed, a grainy black-and-white image showed a boy of perhaps eight, standing solemnly before a clapboard farmhouse with wide eaves and a rail fence. His hair was neatly combed, his expression serious but steady, a huge pumpkin lay on the ground at his feet.

Graham's heart thudded. He reached into his satchel, fumbling, and pulled out the picture he had found with Emilie's letters. He laid it beside the clipping.

The resemblance was undeniable, the same farmhouse, the same boy, though captured from a slightly different angle.

Norma gasped. "It's the same house! The very same. Graham, you already had his picture, and now we know where it was taken."

Graham could barely speak. "This is definitely Lucien then." His eyes stung, and he quickly blinked.

Denise touched the clipping gently. "Now you have not only a name, but a story. He was cared for. He belonged somewhere."

They sat for a long time, absorbing the weight of the discoveries.

Graham finally asked, "Do you know what became of him later?"

Denise shook her head. "No. These early records tell us only so much. If you wish, I can search for later census entries, marriage records. But already we know the beginning, his mother's name, her death, his early home, that his grandparents raised him."

Norma smiled warmly. "That is such a gift. Thank you, Denise."

The archivist inclined her head. "It is my pleasure. Every life deserves to be remembered."

Phil leaned back in his chair. "So, to recap: Lucien Tremblay, born 1893. Mother Émilie Tremblay, who died when he was five. He lived with his grandparents on the Tremblay farm, which we can probably still find. And we have a confirmed photograph."

"Yes," Graham said slowly, his voice thick. "For the first time, he feels real. Not just a name on a page, but a child who stood on the earth, who looked into a camera one afternoon."

Denise carefully slid the newspaper clipping into a protective sleeve and photocopied it for them. She did the same with the baptism and death record, giving Graham tidy copies he could carry.

As she handed them over, she said, "You should visit the farm if you can. Many old Tremblay homesteads still stand in the countryside. Perhaps someone there remembers."

Graham held the papers as if they were fragile treasure. "I will. Thank you."

"And the family will be buried in the churchyard here in the town," she added.

Norma's eyes widened.

They rose, thanked her again, and stepped back into the bright afternoon.

The town stretched before them, bathed in sunlight. The river glimmered in the distance, and the mountains framed the horizon.

For a moment, none of them spoke. Then Phil said softly, "Well. That was a lot."

Norma slipped her arm through Graham's. "How are you feeling?"

Graham exhaled slowly. "Grateful. Saddened. But also ... connected. For the first time, I know his story began here, with Émilie, with the grandparents. He wasn't forgotten. And now he won't be."

Phil clapped him on the back. "And tomorrow, we go find that farmhouse."

Norma looked toward the spire of the church in the distance. "How about a quick visit to the graveyard? See what we can find? We could walk it. It's not that far away."

"But then we'd be walking all around the graveyard and then have to walk back," Phil pointed out.

Norma nodded. "Fair enough. I'll go get the car. Back in a jiffy."

And she was.

The minute Graham and Phil climbed in, she pulled out into the road. "Did you know Baie-Saint-Paul is one of the oldest parishes in Charlevoix. Founded in the seventeenth century. So if François and Marie are buried here, that churchyard has probably seen generations of Tremblays."

Graham sat back, letting the words settle over him. He imagined Émilie as a girl running through these same streets, Lucien as a boy trailing after his grandparents. And knowing his own grandfather lived and worked here for a while made him realize he was seeing the same views that Stuart Brody had seen over a hundred years before. The idea sent a shiver down his spine: their feet had touched this ground, and now his were about to.

The car coasted down the road, the houses tighter now, bright gardens spilling over fences. At the center stood the parish church, a white-stone building with twin steeples pointing skyward. Its bells were silent, but the square around it buzzed with life: tourists snapping photos, locals chatting on benches, the smell of coffee drifting from a nearby café.

"There it is," Norma breathed. "The church from the records. We'll come back if you want, but the graveyard is on the next street. In the old days it was probably all one piece of land." She drove to the back of the church and found an empty parking spot. They could see the cemetery across a small road behind.

"You ready?" Phil asked.

Graham swallowed. "As I'll ever be."

They stepped out, and headed across the road. As they neared the churchyard, Graham felt his pulse quicken. An iron gate opened onto rows of gravestones, some upright and crisp, others leaning and half-swallowed by grass.

"This is it," he said, his voice low.

They entered. The churchyard was quiet except for birdsong and the faint hum of the town beyond. Gravel paths threaded between graves dating back centuries. Some stones were polished granite, their names sharp and clear; others were lichen-covered, their inscriptions barely legible. Crosses leaned toward each other like whispering elders.

Phil unfolded a small notebook. "So, we're looking for François Tremblay, died 1915, age seventy-eight, and Marie Gagnon, his wife, died 1917, age seventy-four. Both buried here, according to the parish register."

Norma shaded her eyes. "Emilie took I'm sure. That narrows it down a little. But there are *a lot* of Tremblays."

Indeed, everywhere Graham looked he saw the name: etched into marble, carved into wood, even painted on small iron crosses. Tremblay after Tremblay, a forest of kin.

"Well," Phil said cheerfully, "at least we're in the right family reunion."

They spread out, weaving between rows. Graham crouched at one stone, brushing moss away. The name appeared: *Joseph Tremblay, époux de Marie Bouchard.* Not the right one. He tried another: *Pierre Tremblay, 1882.* Again, no.

Norma's voice floated over from the next row. "This one's close. François Tremblay, but he died in 1892. Too early."

Graham moved slowly, each stone a question mark. His fingers traced letters carved a century or more before, the grooves worn shallow by rain and time. He imagined someone once standing where he stood, weeping as those names were carved.

Finally, near the back corner of the yard, shaded by an old maple, he stopped. The stone was taller than most, its top carved in a simple arch. The letters, though weathered, were still clear enough to read.

Ici repose François Tremblay, cultivateur, décédé le 14 mars 1915, âgé de 78 ans.

Graham's breath caught. "Here." His voice was little more than a whisper. "I found them."

Phil and Norma hurried over. They stood in silence, three figures before the stone.

"There's more," Graham said, kneeling. Beneath François's inscription was another: *Son épouse, Marie Gagnon, décédée le 2 avril 1917, âgée de 74 ans.*

"They're together," Norma said softly. "But where is Emilie?"

For a long moment, the three simply stood. A light breeze stirred the maple leaves, scattering dappled shadows across the grave.

Graham reached out, his fingers grazing the stone. It was cool, rough, solid. More real than any census record could ever be. "This is them. Lucien's grandparents. They were just names on a screen a few days ago."

Phil put a hand on his shoulder. "Now you've come full circle. From their house, to their records, to their resting place."

Norma knelt, pulling a small notebook from her bag. "Let's write down the exact wording. And I'll take a photo." She snapped a picture with her phone, then carefully copied the inscription. "This way, even if the stone erodes, you'll always have it."

Graham smiled faintly. "Thanks."

Norma pointed to other nearby stones: more Tremblays, some with matching dates suggesting siblings, cousins, children. "This whole section might be their extended family," she mused. She walked away, reading the names of other stones. "She's here! I found Emilie!" She took more pictures.

Graham crouched again, resting his hand on the grass before the grave. He thought of Lucien, running barefoot through fields, his grandparents still alive. He thought of Émilie, a girl in the 1891 census, growing up under her parents' watchful eyes. He thought of the day in 1898 when the family had gathered here to bury her, and then in 1915 for Francois, and finally in 1917 for Marie. It must have been hard for Lucien to lose his close family at such a young age.

Norma touched his arm. "Let's go inside the church. It feels right to step where they worshipped."

The others agreed. They walked back through the churchyard, leaving the graves under the maple's watchful branches. Inside, the church was cool and dim, sunlight filtering through stained glass in hues of blue and gold. Wooden pews stretched in neat rows, polished by centuries of hands.

They sat quietly, each lost in thought. Graham gazed at the altar, trying to picture Lucien and his family kneeling in these very pews, whispering prayers.

When they finally stepped back into the sunlight, the square outside bustled as before. Yet for the three of them, everything felt different, weighted with meaning.

As they returned to the car, Graham glanced back once more at the steeples piercing the sky. "I'd really love to find the family farmhouse," he said. "Walk the Rang Saint-Laurent, maybe find the land they farmed."

Phil grinned. "Sounds like a plan for tomorrow. My feet are killing me, and I need a nap."

Norma laughed. "And maybe stop at that café I smelled earlier. Ancestors and espresso; perfect combination."

They drove out of the square, the church growing smaller behind them, but its presence stayed. The Tremblays were no longer distant names in census margins. They were here: rooted in the soil of Baie-Saint-Paul, remembered by the stones and the air and now by Graham himself.

Chapter Thirteen

The morning light in Paris was soft and golden; the kind of light that made even the busiest streets look like they belonged in a museum. Ellie leaned her head against the train window as the TGV rumbled free of the city, carrying her and Quinn southward toward Limoges. The reflection of her new husband's face caught in the glass; his dark hair slightly mussed from the early start, his smile still a little dazed from croissants and too-strong coffee, and she thought again of how surreal it all felt. Honeymoon. France. Quinn by her side.

She reached for his hand, squeezing once, lightly. He gave her that look she loved, the half-grin that seemed to say both *I can't believe you're mine* and *what are you up to now?*

"Do you realize," Quinn said, stretching his long legs out as best he could, "it's been less than a month since we were saying vows in front of everyone? I feel like the whole world has turned inside out since then."

Ellie laughed softly. "Maybe because we've packed so much into every day. Paris doesn't exactly lend itself to quiet evenings in. Yet we're asleep before most people start supper!"

"No regrets," he replied, glancing out the window as the city suburbs gave way to rolling fields, green and gold under a widening sky. "Not one."

She followed his gaze. The view was changing fast; patches of farmland, the neat geometry of vineyards, a scatter of red-roofed villages whose church steeples rose high in the air. It was different from Paris's grand boulevards and palaces, humbler, but no less lovely. She imagined them slowing down here, strolling through a market, learning the names of cheeses from patient vendors who grinned at their horrible attempts to speak French. She turned, resting her head briefly on his shoulder. The steady rhythm of the train, the scent of coffee still clinging to his shirt, and the warmth of him steadied her.

"You have no idea how thankful I am for you," she murmured. "This whole trip, all the details, the tickets, the hotels. I know it didn't just happen magically. You set it all up. You made it possible."

Quinn laughed softly, a little sheepishly. "Well, I'll confess. I had some help."

She lifted her head, mock-suspicious. "Help?"

"Your Aunt Norma," he admitted. "She's the one who told me which routes to book, which hotels you'd love. She practically had a spreadsheet of recommendations. I just followed orders."

Ellie laughed so loudly a woman across the aisle glanced over, smiling. "That sounds exactly like Norma. She probably color-coded it too."

"Blue for must-sees, green for maybe-if-there's-time," Quinn said, nodding solemnly.

"Red for do-not-bother?" Ellie added, and they both chuckled. The tension that had curled in her chest eased, replaced by warmth. She liked to know ahead of time what they were doing and where they were going. But for once, she let go and put her trust in others. And it was working out just fine.

The train slowed briefly as it passed another station. Ellie glimpsed stone houses with ivy tumbling down their walls, laundry flapping on lines strung between shuttered windows. A boy pedaled a bicycle down a narrow lane, chasing after a dog that bounded ahead. It was a fleeting tableau, gone in seconds, but it made her heart swell.

She turned back to Quinn. "I can't believe we're really doing this. Not just Paris, but all of it. Rivièreclaire, then back again. You've given me... I don't know, a gift of time, of space to breathe. After the chaos of the wedding and everything leading up to it, the Percyville celebration, and losing Lennie, this feels like finally exhaling."

"That's exactly what I wanted," Quinn said simply. His eyes softened. "You give so much, Ellie. You're always looking after everyone else; your family, the Heritage Harvesters, me. I wanted you to have a stretch of days where the only thing you had to do was be happy."

She kissed him then, quick and tender, before leaning back against the seat. Outside, the land was opening up wider, more hills rolling toward the horizon. Here and there a château appeared, pale stone rising above a cluster of trees like a dream of another century.

Ellie thought of Gillian again, digging through family records, piecing together stories. Maybe her mother's family had once lived in a village like this in England, in a house with blue shutters and a garden of lavender. Maybe that was what Gillian was so breathless about; the possibility of finding roots not just in documents but in real places, places they could touch and see.

Quinn's words lingered. *Together.* Whatever came going forward, she wouldn't face it alone.

"Do you think," she asked softly, "that people really carry the past in their bones? That who we are is shaped by people we've never met?"

Quinn considered. "I think we inherit echoes. But how we listen to them, that's up to us."

She let the thought settle in her. The rhythm of the train, steady as a heartbeat, seemed to agree. Fields swept past, orchards heavy with fruit, rivers glinting like silver ribbons. Somewhere in the carriage, a baby gurgled and laughed, its parents whispering in French.

Ellie closed her eyes briefly, memorizing it all; the movement, the sound, the nearness of Quinn. This was what she had always dreamed of, though she hadn't known how much until now: love, and discovery, and a future built not just from the past but in defiance of it, a choice made every day.

When she opened her eyes, Quinn was watching her. "What?" she asked, smiling.

"Just wondering how I got this lucky," he said.

She squeezed his hand again, their fingers weaving together as the train carried them farther south toward whatever awaited them there, and beyond that, back to Paris, to Aunt Gillian's discoveries and all the stories still waiting to be told.

The train slid into Limoges-Bénédictins station just before lunch, its brakes sighing like a long-held breath. Ellie sat up straighter, pressing her hands to the window as the building came into view. "Oh," she whispered. "It looks like a castle."

Quinn leaned closer to see. The station rose with elegant domes and a clock tower, its creamy stone gleaming against the pale sky. Art Nouveau curves framed the windows, and green patina edged the roof. It was more than a train stop; it was a monument.

Quinn grabbed their bag, having left the other at the hotel for their return, and joined the gentle stream of passengers. The tiled concourse echoed with footsteps and the murmurs of travelers. Ellie tilted her head back to take in the soaring ceiling, the ironwork arches, the stained-glass panels that caught the light like fragments of a fairy-tale.

"This doesn't feel like arriving in a city," she said softly. "It feels like being welcomed."

Quinn smiled at her wonder. "Exactly why I wanted us to come here. Not just the big destinations, but places that still surprise you."

Ellie tugged Quinn's sleeve toward the view beyond. He glanced up. "It looks like something out of a storybook. But right now, I'd take a storybook that carries its own luggage."

Outside the station, the square was alive with the hum of taxis pulling in and out, the scent of warm stone and exhaust fumes. Ellie spotted a vacant cab and waved; the driver, a wiry man with silver hair and kind eyes, leaned across to pop the trunk.

“Vous allez où?” he asked. "Where are you going?"

Ellie consulted her phone. “Do you know the town of Rivièreclaire? The address is here.” She passed the screen forward.

The driver gave a small nod of recognition as they all settled inside. “Ah, twenty-five minutes, pas plus. Joli petit village.” He pulled away from the curb, the engine purring as they slipped into the late-day traffic.

Within minutes, Limoges began to thin. Rows of ochre-colored buildings gave way to rolling countryside, fields ribbed with hedgerows and dotted with clusters of cattle. Ellie pressed her face to the window, drinking in every view. Quinn, by contrast, slouched into the seat, arms folded, though a smile tugged at the corner of his mouth when a herd of goats blocked a lane, forcing the taxi to idle.

“This feels unreal,” Ellie whispered.

“Unreal in a good way?” Quinn asked.

“Yes. Like we accidentally booked a holiday in the past.”

The driver chuckled softly, catching Ellie’s words even in English. “C’est vrai. Here, everything is slow. Pas Paris, pas Toulouse. Quiet life.”

As they turned off the main road, the scenery changed again. Low stone walls bordered winding lanes, and the smell of wood smoke drifted faintly from unseen chimneys. A sign painted in fading green letters announced Rivièreclaire, though no one else seemed around to read it.

The village unfolded in a scatter of slate-roofed houses, shutters painted in gentle blues and greens. A narrow bridge arched over the river, its surface worn smooth by centuries of footsteps, while a larger bridge just beyond was for cars. Flowers still clung stubbornly in window boxes, though the air hinted at autumn.

Ellie let out a long breath. “This is perfect.”

Quinn leaned forward, peering through the windshield. “It’s quiet. Really quiet.”

The taxi rolled to a stop before a two-story stone house tucked behind a chestnut tree. The driver stepped out, lifting their bag from the trunk as if it weighed nothing. "Voilà," the driver said with a sweeping hand motion. "You will like it here."

Ellie paid the fare, slipping in a grateful "merci beaucoup." The car pulled away, leaving them with the chorus of crickets and the scent of damp earth.

For a moment neither spoke. Then Quinn lifted the bag onto his shoulder, squinting at the house. "Well," he said, "if the inside is half as pretty as the drive, I might forgive you for dragging me across France."

Ellie laughed at his joke as they walked up the gravel path toward the front door.

The B&B sat slightly outside the main village; a long, two-story farmhouse with worn blue shutters and a wisteria-covered gate. A sign on the fence read: *Les Oiseaux Perdus*. The Lost Birds.

"Seems appropriate," Quinn murmured.

They stepped inside to find a stout woman in her sixties at the front desk. She greeted them with a warm, reserved smile.

"Bonjour," she said. "I am Madame Rousseau, and you must be the Canadians."

Ellie stepped forward. "Yes. Ellie and Quinn."

"You have the room upstairs on the left. It has a delightful view of the old road."

"My ancestor is from this town," Ellie blurted out. The woman narrowed her eyes and Ellie felt a blush creep up her neck.

"What was the name?"

"Leonard Ethier," Ellie mumbled.

Madame Rousseau nodded her head. "Oui, the family used to live here."

Quinn frowned as he filled out the register the woman had set on the reception counter. "There's no one left?" he asked.

She shook her head. "Not for many generations." She spun the book around and looked through her glasses at the information he had provided.

"No one wants to live in a small village anymore, unless they are old, or tourists who visit and think this is the life."

"Did you grow up here?" Ellie asked, wondering if she had some interesting information herself.

Madame Rousseau shook her head. "No. I met my husband in Paris and we moved here, to his hometown." She stared at Ellie for a minute. "My husband was the archivist here until he passed."

"I'm so sorry," Ellie said.

Madame Rousseau nodded, eyes unreadable. "He would have liked your interest in the past. He left behind… too many boxes. Come, let me show you your room."

She led them up a narrow staircase, highly polished dark wooden railings catching the light. The room she opened the door to was modest but charming; exposed beams, lace curtains, an antique desk that creaked when Ellie ran her fingers over it. The view looked out over the orchard and beyond the clustered roofs of the town.

Ellie took her journal from her purse and laid it open on the desk. The entry for Leonard Ethier faced her.

Quinn dropped their bag on the floor. "So, what's the plan?"

Madame Rousseau hovered, then raised a hand. "If you are searching for family, you might want to visit Camille."

Quinn looked up. "Who's Camille?"

"She is in charge of the town's history. Young and very enthusiastic. She will help you."

Ellie smiled. "Thank you, Madame Rousseau."

The older woman shrugged then chuckled. "My father would haunt me to the grave if I didn't help someone looking for family." She motioned to the room. "Settle in. I don't serve lunch but supper is at six o'clock. Camille is there until five o'clock, so you can wander the town for a bit."

Chapter Fourteen

Ellie slipped her arm through Quinn's as they stepped out of the café after lunch. The lingering warmth of roasted chicken, herbed potatoes, and the soft red wine still clung to her, but the fresh air cut through it in the best way. The town felt alive but unhurried, sunlight spilling across narrow cobbled streets that twisted away like ribbons. They had agreed to an hour of exploring before visiting Camille and Ellie's fingers were crossed that the town historian would have access to more information about Leonard Ethier.

"I can't get over how quiet it is," Ellie said, her voice low, though she didn't really need to whisper. "Even with people around, it feels... peaceful."

Quinn smiled, adjusting his sunglasses. "Small towns move at their own pace. France doesn't care if we're used to rushing." He tilted his head toward the row of houses across the street. "Look at that one. Doesn't it feel like something out of a painting?"

It did. A slate roof, the edges softened by moss, sat crooked but proud above walls of pale stone. Shutters the color of faded sage framed the windows, and geraniums spilled red from clay pots on the sills. A hand-painted sign above the doorway read *Boulangerie*, the scent of baking bread drifting faintly even this far.

They wandered on, shoes tapping on uneven stones, the streets narrowing and widening in a pattern Ellie found both confusing and delightful. Some of the houses had been turned into tiny shops; an atelier with watercolor prints hung in a window, a chocolatier with a single round table outside, a bookshop that smelled faintly of leather and ink when they peeked in.

Ellie paused at nearly every doorway, running her fingers along the rough stone or leaning in to catch a whiff of scented bundles tied with twine. She found herself wondering what the place had looked like when her ancestor had walked these same streets. Did he stop here for bread? Did he pause at the fountain in the square to drink, or did he hurry through with his head down, eager to be elsewhere?

The thought lingered as they climbed a gentle slope and came into view of the church. Its steeple was modest, barely cresting above the rooftops, but the slate spire cut neatly into the sky. The stone walls were worn smooth, pale gray with centuries of weather, and the wooden door was heavy, iron hinges curling like vines.

Ellie slowed. "That's it," she whispered, though she wasn't sure why she felt the need to hush her voice. "The church. It has to be the one."

Quinn gave her arm a squeeze. "Let's take a look."

A broken archway marked what was once a grand entrance, now overgrown with ivy and moss. Wildflowers pushed through cracks in the flagstone.

The churchyard gate creaked as they pushed it open, the hinges complaining before settling back into silence. A narrow path, lined with tufts of grass, led them past rows of grave markers. Some were so old their names had worn away entirely, just stones hunched in the earth like tired shoulders. Others stood sharp and clean, polished marble catching the light.

Ellie slowed at each one, scanning the names with a strange mix of anticipation and reverence. Then, about halfway down the row, she froze.

"Quinn. Look."

The stone was simple, the letters carved deeply but softened at the edges by time: *Ethier*. Below it, two first names she didn't recognize. She knelt without thinking, brushing her fingertips across the carved grooves.

Her heart fluttered, caught between excitement and confusion. Ethier. It was her family name, or at least the thread that had led her here, across the ocean and into this tiny town. But she didn't know these given names, couldn't place them in the tangle of stories she'd pieced together from records and fading photographs.

Quinn crouched beside her, reading silently. After a moment, he placed a hand lightly on her shoulder. "We'll have to come back," he said gently. "Give it time. Maybe Camille can find some information for you."

Ellie nodded, though her throat felt tight. "It's just... strange. To see it here. To know this is real."

They lingered a little longer, wandering the paths in silence. Ellie found two more Ethier stones, each one tugging at her heart with questions she couldn't yet answer. At last, they made their way out through the gate and back into the streets.

The town welcomed them as if nothing had changed, though Ellie carried the quiet weight of the graveyard with her. They passed into a square where a few open-air shops had set out tables laden with wares. An elderly woman stood behind a stall of embroidered linens, smiling as Ellie ran her hand over a delicate table runner stitched with lavender sprigs.

"For your Aunt Jenny?" Quinn asked, already reaching for his wallet.

Ellie smiled. "She'll love it."

At the next stall, Quinn found a set of hand-carved wooden spoons. "My sister, Bonnie, would use these every day in Gran's place in Montreal," he said, holding them up. The vendor beamed when Quinn purchased them, carefully wrapping them in paper.

They drifted from table to table, the afternoon warming around them. Ellie picked up small jars of honey for her cousin, Quinn chose a leather notebook for his father, and together they sampled candied almonds dusted with sugar that clung to their fingers. The townspeople greeted them warmly, patient when Ellie stumbled over her French, kind enough to laugh softly rather than frown.

By the time their bags felt pleasantly heavy with more gifts for family and friends, they'd wandered down toward the river. A small park spread out along the bank; benches set beneath chestnut trees whose leaves were just beginning to turn at the edges. Quinn steered them toward one that overlooked the water.

The river moved slowly, a mirror of the blue sky, the occasional ripple catching sunlight like scattered coins. Across the way, fields stretched toward the horizon, green giving way to gold.

Ellie sank onto the bench with a sigh, setting the shopping bags at her feet. "I think I could sit here forever."

Quinn leaned back, stretching one arm along the top of the bench. "Not a bad place to catch your breath, is it?"

For a while they sat in comfortable silence, the murmur of the river and the distant chatter of children playing filling the air. A breeze carried the faint scent of cut grass and something floral Ellie couldn't quite place.

Finally, Ellie spoke, her voice thoughtful. "It feels like I've stepped into another life. Like part of me belongs here, even though I've never been before."

Quinn glanced at her, his expression soft. "Maybe part of you does. Blood has a long memory."

She smiled at that, resting her head lightly against his shoulder. The curiosity of not knowing exactly how the names in the graveyard connected to her family remained. Waiting to be uncovered.

The town around them seemed to breathe, content and steady. The river rolled on, as it always had, as it always would. Ellie closed her eyes, letting the peace of it sink into her bones.

"We'll come back," Quinn said quietly, almost to himself. "But now, we should go see what Camille can find for you."

Ellie grinned. The thought of solving this family mystery sent a butterfly swooping through her stomach. For some people it was climbing the tallest mountains. For Ellie, it was finding an ancestor, knowing their story, and setting them in place in her family tree.

***

A church bell tolled as Ellie and Quinn arrived at the building where the municipal records were kept. The building had once been a one-room schoolhouse, its old blackboards now leaning behind stacks of acid-free boxes. Inside, a young woman stood over a scanner, placing photos of brittle parish records on the screen then gently returning them to their folders. She wore a gray wool sweater rolled at the sleeves; her brown hair tied back in a messy knot.

She glanced up and smiled, walking towards them with her hand outstretched. "You must be Ellie, looking for the Ethier family," she said. "I am Camille Durand. Not a mind reader. Madame Rousseau called to say you would be by and what you're looking for. I've been waiting for you. And I think I found something!" Her accent was heavy, but her English was perfect.

Ellie offered her hand. "I'm glad to meet you as well. But I must admit I'm a bit overwhelmed."

Camille held up a hand as if to say, not to worry, and gestured toward the cluttered back half of the archive where a desk sat empty save for a couple of file folders and three chairs placed around it. "I cleared a spot for you. It's not glamorous. This town's budget hasn't changed since 1983."

"It's perfect," Ellie said as they all took a seat. "I guess Madame Rousseau also told you who in particular I'm looking for?"

Camille nodded. "She mentioned the name Léonard Ethier, and I've only found one here in Rivièreclaire."

"He was a shoemaker and left France in 1665 to go to Canada. I'm trying to find out why he left in the first place," Ellie said. "I may never find that information, but if anyone might know something, it might be you."

Camille pushed her glasses up the bridge of her nose, and carefully opened the folder. "I think I have found why he left, and he was quite lucky, actually. He's mentioned in conjunction with the move of settlers to New France under Jean Talon, and..." she hesitated, reread the document and frowned. She looked up. "It's very sad."

Ellie leaned in. The document inside was a single sheet of parchment, the ink browned with age but still legible in the clerk's hand. It was held safe in an acid-free plastic sleeve. At the top was the date: 1663.

Camille traced a finger just above the words. "Here. I'll translate for you. *'A grievous fire broke out in the shop of Leonard Ethier, shoemaker. His wife, Anne, and son, Gaston, being inside at the time, perished. The workshop was lost, but the house remained.'*" She looked up, frowning. "It's chilling, isn't it? Two lives lost, but remembered here in a few stark lines."

Ellie's throat tightened. She had grown used to the dry, factual tone of archives, but reading about a man losing his family like this, three centuries ago and yet immediate on the page, was different. "Do you know where he lived?"

"Oh, yes," Camille said brightly, already reaching for another folder. "I looked it up as well. Leonard Ethier owned the house at the corner of Beauchamps and Grenier. You've passed it, I'm sure. It's still standing, though, of course, much altered."

Ellie exchanged a glance with Quinn, who had been leaning back in his seat, arms crossed. His brows lifted, amused at Camille's thoroughness.

"You've done your homework," Ellie said.

Camille gave a little shrug, though she looked pleased. "I couldn't resist. When I heard what you were looking for, I wanted to be sure I could tell you the rest of the story. It was a welcome break. And..." She hesitated, then admitted, "I called ahead. I hope you don't mind. The woman who owns the house now is a friend of mine. I told her you might pass by, and she said if you stopped, she'd be glad to show you around."

Ellie blinked at her. "You... called ahead?"

Camille shrugged. "I know everyone," she said simply, a smile tugging her mouth. "Town historian by day, social networker by night."

Quinn chuckled. "That settles it then. We'd better go pay her a visit."

***

The afternoon sunlight slanted golden through the narrow streets as Ellie and Quinn made their way toward Beauchamps and Grenier. The air smelled faintly of woodsmoke and damp stone, and every house they passed seemed to have its own secret, its own centuries of lives stacked one atop another.

"There," Ellie said softly when the house came into view. It was small, a tidy two-story cottage with pale plaster walls and dark beams showing through, the roof pitched steeply against the weight of the coming winter snow. Flower boxes brightened the windows, and a bicycle leaned casually against the fence.

Quinn slowed beside her. "I'm glad the house survived the fire."

"Me too." She pictured Leonard Ethier's workshop, the glow of lamplight on leather, the smell of hides and oil; and then smoke, screams, the frantic rush to save what couldn't be saved. The image lingered as they reached the gate.

The door opened before they could knock. A woman stepped out, smiling warmly, wiping flour from her hands onto an apron. "You must be Ellie and Quinn. Camille told me to expect you. I'm Sylvie."

Ellie returned the smile, struck at once by the easy hospitality. "Thank you for letting us intrude."

"Not at all," Sylvie said, her impeccable English welcome to hear. "Come in, come in. I love sharing the history of the place."

Inside, the house was a surprise. The rooms were small, with low ceilings and narrow doorways, but everything gleamed. A modern kitchen opened off the entry, filled with light and warmth. The sitting room had exposed beams, a fireplace, and shelves crammed with books. Ellie felt instantly at ease, as though the house were alive and glad to have company.

"I renovated a few years ago," Sylvie explained as she led them through. "Tried to keep the charm but make it livable. You know how it is with old houses, quirks everywhere."

"They give it character," Quinn said, running a hand along the uneven plaster wall.

Sylvie's eyes brightened. "Oh, you'll appreciate this, then. I kept one original feature upstairs. Follow me."

They climbed the narrow staircase, the steps creaking pleasantly underfoot. In the attic, sunlight slanted through a dormer window, catching on a single beam left exposed amid the clean white plaster. The wood was dark with age, worn smooth except for two sets of initials carved deep into the grain.

"Leonard Ethier," Sylvie said softly. "And just beside it, Anne, his wife. The carving predates the fire, obviously. I found it during the renovation and couldn't bear to cover it up."

Ellie stepped closer, her chest tightening again. The letters were crude but determined, pressed into the beam by hands long vanished. She imagined the young couple, perhaps standing together one quiet evening, laughing as they carved their names. A promise in wood.

Quinn moved beside her, tilting his head. "You know," he murmured, "people change their clothes, their houses, their tools. Centuries pass. But lovers..." He touched the carved initials gently before taking out his phone and snapping pictures. "Lovers never change. They always want to leave their mark somewhere."

Ellie swallowed hard, blinking back an unexpected sting of tears. It was true. Across time, across tragedy, the impulse was the same: to say *we were here, we belonged to each other.*

Sylvie smiled softly at them both, as though she understood. "It's my favorite part of the house. Makes me feel like I'm sharing it with them."

They lingered a little longer, admiring the attic and then the garden out back, where herbs grew in neat rows where the workshop had once stood. Quinn took over the job of documenting the visit with copious photographs, as he could see Ellie was deep in the past. When at last they stepped out into the street again, having thanked Sylvie for her kindness with two strangers, the light had changed, evening was easing forward.

Ellie walked in silence for a while; her thoughts caught between past and present. At last she said, "I can't stop thinking about how something so devastating, fire, loss, left behind not just ashes, but this... continuity. Their names, their love, preserved under a roof that still shelters people today."

Quinn gave her hand a gentle squeeze. "That's the thing about history, isn't it? It isn't just what's written in the archives. It's the lives still echoing through the beams, the bricks, the soil. And sometimes, if we're lucky, we get to feel it."

Ellie nodded, the image of Leonard and Anne's initials carved in oak burning steady in her mind. The past wasn't gone; it was simply waiting to be noticed.

Chapter Fifteen

The smell of breakfast drifted up the staircase of the B&B in Baie-Saint-Paul the next morning, coaxing the three travelers from their rooms. Downstairs, Madeleine bustled about the dining room, setting out baskets of croissants and bowls of fresh fruit. The morning light poured through lace curtains, pooling across the polished wooden table.

"Bon matin!" she sang out as they entered. "Did you sleep well?"

"Like a stone," Phil said, grabbing a croissant with exaggerated reverence.

Norma slid gracefully into her chair, smoothing her cardigan. "Madeleine, this house is so peaceful. I could stay a month."

Graham, though, looked distracted. He spooned sugar into his coffee with unusual care.

Madeleine noticed. "You went to see Denise, yes? Did she help?"

"Yes," Graham said quietly. "More than I ever imagined. She found records of Lucien's birth ... and of his mother's death when he was just five. And a newspaper clipping showing him at the farmhouse with his grandparents."

Madeleine's eyes softened. "Ah. That is a hard story, but also a gift. You have family here."

Phil swallowed a mouthful of bread. "So today we're going to find that farmhouse, right?"

Madeleine nodded. "Of course. I did a little snooping last night. Okay, I called Denise, and through her connections we found out where the old Tremblay homestead is. A few kilometers outside town, on the road toward Petite-Rivière-Saint-François. The house is still standing. For the past years it's been rented out to families, but the last one left about three months ago. And the land around is rented to neighbours for crops."

Graham's heart gave a leap.

Norma reached across and touched Graham's hand. "We'll go after breakfast, then."

***

The road narrowed as they left the highway, following Madelaine's directions carefully, climbing slightly, bordered by wide pastures dotted with round hay bales. Cows grazed lazily, tails swishing, while beyond them the Saint Lawrence shimmered silver in the distance. Old barns leaned against the horizon, their paint long faded but their bones still strong.

"This is it," Norma murmured, almost reverently. "This is their world."

Phil slowed the car. The street sign appeared at last: *Rang Saint-Laurent.* Just a simple green rectangle.

They turned onto the road. It was quiet, just a few cars passing. Wooden houses stood back from the road, some freshly painted, others faded and sagging with age. Fields stretched behind them, stitched with stone walls.

Graham pressed his forehead to the glass, drinking it all in. He tried to imagine François and Marie in 1901, standing on this very road, greeting neighbors, hauling milk to town. Émilie as a teenager, her skirts brushing the dust. Lucien as a boy, chasing after a runaway chicken.

Norma consulted her notes. "Okay. The 1901 census lists them as on Rang Saint-Laurent, lot number 37. Madelaine said it's five minutes from the highway, red barn in front of a white farmhouse with green trim."

"On the right-hand side of the road," Graham added.

Phil slowed as they neared the five-minute mark, then pulled off the road. He gestured across a wide field that sloped gently toward the river. The farmhouse stood in the distance, a weathered red-roofed barn beside it.

Graham stared, hardly breathing. "That's their farm." The words felt both daring and inevitable.

Norma squinted into the sunlight. "Want to take a walk?" She got out and waited for the others to join her.

They walked up the dirt lane, shoes crunching on gravel, until the white farmhouse rose out of the quiet like a ship on a pale sea. The paint was still bright in the early morning sun, but here and there a shutter sagged or the trim had peeled away in curling flakes. Graham slowed first, hands tucked in his pockets, and gave a half-smile.

"Feels strange," he said, looking at the empty porch. "Like someone just stepped away and forgot to come back."

Norma tilted her head, peering up at the curtained windows. The curtains had faded to the color of parchment, but they still hung neatly, as if waiting for someone to tug them open. "It's neat, though," she murmured. "It's smart to use as a rental. Though it looks abandoned, or maybe just... sleeping."

Phil boldly climbed the stairs to the porch and paused at a side window. He cupped his hands to the glass. "It's fully furnished," he reported. "Someone left a mug on the counter. Must've been the renters." He stepped back, brushing dust from his palms. "Looks like a set for a play that's between acts."

They rounded the farmhouse together, moving slow, each pulled by curiosity. At the back, the garden spread out in a square of tangled green. Wire fencing leaned inward as though tired of holding the place, and the rows were swallowed by waist-high weeds. Yet between the weeds grew a stubborn cluster of herbs; chives pushing purple blossoms, mint spilling dark and aromatic. Norma bent, rubbed a leaf between her fingers, and breathed in. "Still alive," she grinned. "Nature doesn't quit just because no one's looking."

Graham kept his eyes on the far line of trees beyond the garden. A thin row of maples and birch drew a neat division, and past them stretched the golden-green shimmer of cornfields. "Those'll be the rented-out fields Madeline mentioned," he said.

Phil drifted toward the weathered barn a few yards away, its wide doors closed but not flush, a black seam cutting through the sunlit planks. The others followed. The air smelled of dry wood and iron.

"Think it's safe?" Norma asked, though her feet were already carrying her closer.

Graham shrugged. "We're just looking."

They leaned, one after another, to peer through the narrow crack. Inside the barn was shadow and dust, a muted glint of tools left hanging, a coil of rope on a beam. The outlines of an old tractor sat slumped in the half-light like some retired beast. Birdsong echoed inside, hollow.

Phil let out a low whistle. "Hasn't been touched in years."

Graham pressed his forehead briefly against the wood. The barn smelled like his childhood: hay, oil, long summers. He stepped back quickly, before the feeling sank too deep. He pulled out the picture of Lucien and gravitated to the spot where the young boy had stood when the photograph was taken.

"Stay right there!" Norma called out. She had been snapping pictures of the homestead as they walked, and now captured Graham with the sun bouncing off the St. Lawrence in the background, a smile on his face, looking ten years younger. "Now you and Lucien are documented for the future."

They stood there a moment longer, the farmhouse behind them, the fields stretching endlessly ahead. The quiet was not empty, it held the memory of work and living, the faint hum of things paused but not gone.

Norma broke the silence with a soft laugh. "Feels like the land is holding its breath."

Graham nodded. "Yeah. Waiting."

As they stepped back into the sunlight, a figure was approaching along the dirt lane. An older woman, dressed in a sunhat, overalls, and sturdy shoes, moved quickly towards them. She paused when she saw them.

"Bonjour," she called, curious. "You are visiting the Tremblay home? Denise called to say you might."

Norma rolled her eyes. "Does everyone know everyone here?"

The woman laughed. "A friend of a friend knows everyone."

"Yes," Graham said quickly. "I'm ... connected to the family. My half-uncle, Lucien Tremblay, grew up here."

The woman's face brightened with recognition. "Ah, Lucien! I remember him well. And I remember his children, too. He moved away to Montréal many years ago, but he used to come back to visit when I was a girl."

Norma clasped her hands. "You knew him?"

She nodded. "I am Marguerite Desrosiers. Our farm is just beyond the trees. My parents were neighbors to the Tremblays. Lucien was a quiet man, yes, but very kind. He married his first wife here. When she died, he moved his family to Montréal. We heard he remarried and had another son there."

Graham felt his breath hitch. "We know of one son, Rene."

"Yes. After he moved, he would bring them here in the summers sometimes. They ran through these fields, laughing. My mother always said Lucien carried a sadness from losing his mother so young, but with his children he found joy."

Phil glanced at Graham, eyes wide. "So, he has more than one descendant. Living family in Montréal."

Marguerite adjusted her basket. "If you wish, I can fetch my brother, Armand. He remembers more details; names, perhaps."

Fifteen minutes later, Marguerite drove up the driveway with an older man in the passenger seat. He eased out of the car, was stooped but strong, his hands rough from farming. Armand Desrosiers greeted them with a firm handshake.

"Lucien Tremblay," he said in a gravelly voice. "Yes, I remember him. He was older than me, but when I was a boy, he sometimes came back here to help with the harvest. He always had a song on his lips, old chansons, you know? And when he brought his children, ah, how proud he was."

"Do you remember their names?" Graham asked eagerly.

Armand frowned in thought. "The eldest boy ... Rene, I think. His first wife died. It was a sad time. He also has a daughter, Marie. Perhaps another son, Paul? They were from his second marriage It has been long years. But I know they settled in Montréal. I believe Lucien worked at the rail yards."

Norma scribbled the names in her notebook, her hand steady. "Rene, Marie, Paul. Montréal. Rail yards."

Graham felt lightheaded. The pieces of the puzzle were falling into place faster than he could absorb them.

Armand added, "I remember how this farmhouse was always a gathering place. Even after it emptied, no one wanted to sell. It still belongs to the Tremblays. Perhaps one day, someone in the family will return and live here."

Marguerite and Armand left them with promises of more stories if needed.

Finally, Norma broke the stillness. "Should we drive the rest of the road? See where it leads?"

They climbed back into the car and rolled onward, past more farmhouses, barns leaning rakishly, vegetable gardens bursting with late beans and squash. Children riding bicycles along the gravel shoulders, their laughter echoing.

At one bend the road crested a hill, and the view opened wide: the Saint Lawrence gleaming vast and endless, mountains rising blue on the far shore. The sight stole their breath.

"Imagine waking up to this every morning," Graham murmured.

"No wonder they stayed," Norma said softly.

Phil parked at a small lookout, and they stepped out again. The wind was stronger here, tugging at their clothes. Graham felt both very small and profoundly connected. Lucien and his family had stood on this land, gazed at this same river. The horizon they knew was the one he saw now.

Norma opened her notebook, jotting quickly. "Okay. So we've got: Lot 37, Rang Saint-Laurent, census confirmed. Gravestones in the parish churchyard. Parish records for death dates. That's a solid trail." She looked up, smiling. "You've anchored your family in a place, Graham. That's huge."

He swallowed hard, eyes still on the river. "I never thought I'd feel connected to people I've never met, or even knew about until a few days ago. And now they're not just names, but people. They laughed here. Worked here. Got tired, got hungry, worried about money, dreamed of better harvests. And then they died, and the world went on. And a hundred years later, here I am, standing in their fields."

Phil clapped his shoulder gently. "That's the gift, isn't it? Genealogy isn't only about numbers and charts. It's about putting skin back on the bones of history."

They lingered until the sun was straight above them, its heat warming their bones. Then they drove slowly back toward town, the road unfurling behind them like a ribbon of memory.

As they passed once more by the church steeple, Graham glanced at it and whispered, "I'll be back."

Neither Phil nor Norma asked to whom he spoke; the church, the graves, or the ancestors themselves. The meaning was clear enough.

Chapter Sixteen

Graham, Norma, and Phil had barely crossed the threshold of the bed-and-breakfast after a quick lunch at the café, when the familiar fragrance of lemon polish met them. Madeleine, sleeves rolled up and apron tied, was dusting the baseboards of the dining room, her small frame bustling with energy. She straightened at once when she caught sight of them, her feather duster forgotten in her hand.

"Ah! You are back!" she exclaimed, her voice bright and urgent, as if she had been waiting all morning for their return. She bustled toward them, her eyes darting from Graham's face to Norma's and then to Phil's. "You must tell me everything. Did you find it? The farmhouse?"

Graham gave a weary smile. His shoulders sagged with the weight of discovery, but he couldn't bring himself to dampen her excitement. "Yes, we found it," he said softly. "The farmhouse is still there, and looks like you could move right in. And we met with Marguerite and Armand Desrosiers. They remembered my great-uncle Lucien from when they were children."

Madeleine clasped her hands together and drew in a sharp breath. "How wonderful! Sit, sit, all of you. I will make tea. Tell me everything."

They exchanged quick glances. Norma raised a brow as if to say *we promised ourselves a nap,* but Graham gave the smallest of shrugs. How could they refuse? Madeleine had been nothing but generous and encouraging, her own passion for history fueling their search.

Reluctantly, they sat at the polished oak table, its lace runner freshly pressed. In moments, Madeleine set down a tray with cups and a steaming pot, her eagerness palpable. She leaned forward, elbows resting on the table, chin propped in her hands.

Phil, always the one to break tension, chuckled. “Careful, Madeleine, if you lean any closer, you’ll fall right into the teacups.”

She laughed but didn’t shift back. “Never mind me. I want every detail.”

So Graham began, his voice growing steadier as he painted the picture: the quiet of the land, the inside ready for the next occupant, the barn unused and dusty. He described Marguerite’s and Armand’s memories of Lucien. How Marguerite remembered Lucien as a young man, kind to everyone, losing his first wife and moving his family to Montreal, where he found a second wife and continued his family.

“They said he left for Montréal in the late 1920s,” Graham explained, stirring his tea absently. “He used to bring his family back for summers and the children played in the fields. But their main home was Montreal.”

At this, Madeleine’s face lit with unmistakable triumph. “Then your search is not finished,” she declared, her voice almost musical. She sat upright, her eyes gleaming with excitement. “Now you must go to Montréal, to find his descendants. Perhaps they still live there.”

The words hung in the air like an invitation, and a challenge. Graham felt the stirring of both anticipation and fatigue. The farmhouse had felt like a destination, but now it seemed merely a waypoint. Montreal loomed ahead, its history-rich neighborhoods, its parish records, its cemeteries, and, perhaps, a living branch of his family tree.

Norma, ever the pragmatist, spoke first. “That’s a big city, Madeleine. Montreal isn’t like this village, where everyone knows everyone else.”

Madeleine’s lips curved into a knowing smile. “No, but genealogy has its paths. You begin with what you know, then follow the records. In Québec, the Catholic Church kept meticulous baptismal, marriage, and burial records. Each parish has its archives. And Montreal has many societies devoted to family history. Someone there will help you.”

Phil leaned back, arms crossed. "Sounds like we'll have more research to do when we get home."

Madeleine reached out, touching Graham's hand lightly. "Do you not see? You are walking in your ancestor's footsteps. Lucien left here with hope in his heart. He planted roots in Montreal. If you find his descendants, you will know the path your family took across the years. That is the gift of genealogy; it makes the past live again through the present."

The room fell quiet at her words. Norma's skeptical expression softened, and even Phil gave a small nod. Graham felt something tighten in his chest, a mingling of fear and exhilaration.

"I suppose," he said slowly, "the next step would be parish records. Marguerite believed Lucien married in Montreal. If we could find his marriage record, it would list his wife and possibly their parents. From there, we can trace their children."

Madeleine's eyes danced. "Yes! And do not forget census records. The 1931 census will be a huge help. If Lucien was in Montreal by then, he and his family would be listed. That would tell you their address, their occupations, even the names of their children."

Phil grinned. "Sounds like we're trading sightseeing for record-chasing."

They laughed, but the mood was no longer weary. A sense of purpose filled the room, fueled by Madeleine's passion and their own dawning excitement.

"Madeleine," Graham said after a pause, "how do you know so much about genealogy?"

Norma piped up before the woman could answer. "Remember, her late husband was the town archivist."

Madeleine's smile softened. "I enjoyed sitting nearby while he worked. He loved to tell tales and was interested in new technology. I prefer to work with my hands; he loved the clicking of his keyboard and how it connected him with the world. To me, it is like a great tapestry, and each person is a thread. Your Lucien, he is one of those threads. You are only now seeing where it leads."

Graham's throat tightened. He had thought this trip would be about names and dates, but Madeleine was right, it was about connection, about understanding the lives behind the records. Lucien had not been just a name on a document; he had been a young man who battled adversity and carved out a life in Montreal. And somewhere, perhaps only a few hours' drive away, members of his family might still be living.

He closed his eyes briefly, imagining knocking on a door in Montreal, being greeted by a stranger who might share his eyes or his smile. Would they welcome him? Would they even know Lucien's story?

Madeleine, sensing his quiet hesitation, gave his hand another squeeze. "Do not fear what you might find. Family is family, even across years and oceans. You have already come so far. Montreal is only the next chapter."

Norma pushed back her chair, her practicality reasserting itself. "Well, if Montreal is next, we'll need rest tonight. Tomorrow, we head home to do some online research and see what we can find. But for now," she said, glancing at Graham with a pointed look, "that nap is sounding better than ever."

Madeleine laughed and stood, collecting the empty cups. "Go, go! You have earned your rest. But promise me, you will not stop now. The farmhouse was only the beginning. Montreal will give you the answers you seek."

As they climbed the narrow staircase toward their rooms, Graham felt the exhaustion pressing on him again, but it was lighter now, softened by purpose. The journey was far from over. And somewhere, perhaps a family existed who had no idea they shared blood with him, yet.

***

After spending the rest of the day visiting small shops and having a light supper, they had returned to the B&B to spend their final night before heading home.

Graham sat at the desk in his room and spread the copies from the archives alongside Norma's notes: Émilie's death record, the baptism entry, the newspaper clipping, the neighbors' memories of Lucien's visits and his children.

He whispered the names aloud, tasting them. "Rene. Marie. Paul."

Norma knocked and peeked in. "You're still awake?"

"Yes. I keep thinking ... he wasn't alone. He had children, a life, a legacy."

She smiled softly. "And you're about to bring those threads back together."

Phil appeared at the door with three glasses of wine. "Our host was most gracious in supplying this for us. One last toast before we start planning the next leg of this journey."

They gathered around the desk, glasses raised.

"To Lucien," Graham said, steady now. "And to finding the family he left behind."

Their glasses clinked, and in the quiet of the B&B, with the St. Lawrence murmuring faintly outside, the promise of the next step shone like a lantern before them.

Chapter Seventeen

The rain had pattered against the B&B's windows all night, but finally let up as Graham steered the car home the next morning; the rolling green hills of Charlevoix retreating behind them like a watercolor painting that had smudged into the horizon. The trip to Baie-Saint-Paul had been lovely, artistic, and full of cobblestones Norma had sworn would trip her into an early grave. Now, with suitcases packed into the trunk and a cooler filled with sandwiches and drinks provided by Madeleine, the trio of seniors were making their way back to Percyville.

"Don't get me wrong," Phil said from the passenger seat, his voice a gravelly baritone softened by a restless sleep. "That town is picturesque. But I'll tell you one thing, my hips are going to file a formal complaint. Those sidewalks were designed by sadists."

Norma chuckled from the backseat. "Nonsense, Phil. They were designed by monks in the seventeenth century who clearly believed everyone should walk on cobblestones to toughen their souls. And in your case, maybe your hips."

"Very funny," Phil muttered, tugging at his Montreal Canadiens cap. "You wait until you're my age, Norma."

"You're only six months older than me," she shot back, leaning her head against the head rest.

"Six months is six months. Don't trivialize it."

Graham grinned at the wheel. He was the quiet one of the trio this morning; a careful driver with a soft spot for detours. His family used to joke he had the soul of a cartographer, never going in a straight line when a scenic route presented itself. He was already eyeing the next highway sign, something about Trois-Rivières, when a smaller brown heritage sign caught his attention.

"Hey," he said, pointing with his chin. "Says there's an old seigneurial manor just off the next exit. Open for visitors."

"Oh Lord," Phil groaned. "Not another church or old house."

Norma perked up, her wit sharpening. "What's the matter, Phil? Afraid you'll discover your long-lost ancestors were aristocrats and you'll have to start wearing lace collars?"

"Please," Phil said, "the only thing my ancestors left me is flat feet and a suspicious tolerance for salted pork."

Graham chuckled. "It says the place has a genealogy archive. Could be interesting."

Norma straightened in her seat. "Genealogy, you say? Let's go. Worst case, we learn nothing. Best case, we discover one of you two is descended from pirates, or possibly sheep thieves."

Phil gave her a long-suffering look. "I'd bet on the sheep thieves."

And so, with the kind of impulsive decision-making only road trips encourage, Graham flicked on the turn signal and guided the car down the exit ramp.

The manor was a stately old thing, perched on a gentle rise overlooking the river. Its stone walls gleamed faintly in the afternoon light, and its roofline was tipped with the kind of steep gables that spoke of centuries-old French craftsmanship. A tidy gravel path led up to the door, where a plaque in both English and French welcomed visitors to the *Maison du Seigneur de Castonguay*.

"Castonguay," Norma repeated as they shuffled up the path and inside. "Doesn't that just sound like the name of someone who'd own all the land and charge you rent for grazing your goats? *'Excuse me, monsieur, but you owe three chickens in rent this year.'*"

Inside, an enthusiastic young guide greeted them, barely out of her teens and radiating the kind of cheerfulness that made Norma mutter under her breath about youth being wasted on the young.

"Bonjour! Welcome to the manor," the guide said brightly, obviously having picked up on Norma's English comments. "Would you like to tour the house first, or perhaps visit the genealogy room?"

Phil was ready to veto the entire excursion and head back to the car for a nap, but Norma raised an eyebrow. "Let's do the tour. We should know what kind of aristocrats we're dealing with before we rifle through their paperwork."

The guide's smile widened. "Excellent choice. Right this way."

They followed her into a wide hall with exposed beams and heavy wooden furniture polished to a mirror shine. The young guide clasped her hands and began her spiel.

"This manor was built in the early eighteenth century by the seigneur of Castonguay. The seigneurial system was a form of landholding imported from France. The King granted a seigneur a large tract of land, and in return the seigneur promised to settle it. He would rent long, narrow strips of farmland to families, called *censitaires*. They paid annual dues, sometimes money, sometimes produce, sometimes chickens, and were obliged to help maintain roads and mills."

Phil gave a low whistle. "So basically, feudalism with snow."

The guide chuckled. "That's one way to put it. But it did encourage settlement. By the mid-1700s, the St. Lawrence Valley was filled with these narrow farm lots, each family with access to the river."

Norma squinted at a framed map showing those ribbon-shaped plots. "Ingenious, really. Everyone gets water access; nobody gets stuck with the swamp at the back. Although if I'd lived here, I'd probably have been fined within a week for sneaking onto someone else's lot to steal apples."

Phil muttered, "Or eggs."

They moved into the dining room, where a long table was set with pewter dishes and a loaf of fake bread that looked suspiciously like Styrofoam.

"The seigneur was expected to live here part of the time," the guide explained. "He collected dues but also provided a mill for grinding flour, and sometimes a chapel or school."

"Sounds like being a landlord, priest, and mayor rolled into one," Graham observed.

"Exactly. It was a paternalistic system, though many habitants valued their independence. They didn't always pay on time."

Norma tapped the table. "I imagine there were heated dinner conversations about that. *'Pass the turnips, dear, and by the way, the Tremblays still owe us three sacks of wheat.'*"

The guide giggled. "You'd be surprised how many disputes are recorded in the archives. People argued about fences, pigs wandering, even who had the right to fish in certain streams."

Phil crossed his arms. "Human nature doesn't change much, does it? Still arguing about fences in Percyville."

They toured the kitchen with its iron stove, the small chapel with worn hymnals, and a study lined with books and maps. The manor had an air of quiet authority, but also the faint hum of lives once lived, children running down halls, servants lugging firewood, seigneurs tallying dues.

Finally, the guide led them toward a side room filled with binders and microfilm machines. "And here is our genealogy center. You're welcome to browse. We have baptism, marriage, and burial records, as well as notarial deeds. Many visitors come here to trace their family history."

After discovering that the seniors were only explorers, and not searching for specific family at this time, the guide returned with three large books she thought they'd be interested in. "These are copies, but still quite old." Norma thanked her, and the young woman left the room.

"So," Graham said, carefully opening a register of baptisms. "Who wants to start?"

"Not me," Phil said immediately. "If I find out I'm related to someone important, I'll never hear the end of it from Norma. And if I find out I'm related to criminals, I'll never hear the end of it from Norma."

Norma clasped her hands like a stage actress. "My reputation precedes me. But honestly, isn't it fascinating? These people lived and loved and worked centuries ago, and here we are, nosing around their paperwork."

"It's only fascinating until you realize your great-great-great-grandfather named all his sons Joseph," Phil muttered. "Then it's just confusing."

Graham grinned. "He's got a point."

Norma tilted her head. "Do you suppose they knew they were being confusing? *'Let's all be named Jean-Baptiste, that'll make future genealogists tear their hair out.'*"

The guide reappeared, holding a copy of a map. "Sometimes it helps to trace land ownership. Families stayed tied to the same plots for generations."

They all leaned forward to stare at the names written on long plots of land. Norma used a finger to trace backwards and found Baie-Saint-Paul, then zeroed in on a plot with the name Tremblay in the exact location of his family's farmhouse.

"Here's your family, Graham!" She poked the paper with her nail. "Just where we were yesterday. And this map is dated what?"

The guide squinted at the top and read the date. "1827".

Graham raised an eyebrow and Norma chuffed with pleasure. "Can I take a photo of this?" she asked the guide.

The young lady handed her the document. "These are for sale, if you'd like."

Norma whipped out her purse and handed over the money. Then she passed the map to Graham. "You'll have to add this to your records."

Phil had returned to the ledgers and let out a breath. "Look at this. This family here had fourteen children. Fourteen!"

Norma shook her head. "Can you imagine the laundry?"

Graham whistled. "That explains why people had such big farms. You needed acres just to dry the washing."

They chuckled, but as they flipped through the records, the dry names and dates began to conjure images: families huddled through winter, children baptized in tiny parish churches, widows remarrying to keep farms running. None of it related to them personally, but the weight of history pressed softly around them, like the creak of floorboards in an old house.

Norma tapped a page of entries within a court book with her finger. "Here's a fellow who was fined for hunting on seigneurial land without permission. See, Phil? Sheep thieves were just the beginning. We've got poachers, too."

Phil rolled his eyes. "Don't give her ammunition, Graham. She'll be calling me 'Poacher Phil' all the way home."

Norma grinned wickedly. "Poacher Phil. Has a ring to it, doesn't it?"

After another twenty minutes of poking through binders and teasing each other, their energy flagged. Graham's eyes blurred from squinting at old handwriting, Phil had started yawning conspicuously, and Norma stretched her arms with a groan.

"Goodness," she said. "I thought poring over history would make me feel young and sprightly. Instead, I feel like I've aged fifty years in fifty minutes."

Phil leaned back in his chair, rubbing his knees. "You don't look a day over seventy-five."

"Careful," she shot back. "I still have enough strength left to whack you with this baptismal register."

Graham closed his binder with a decisive thump. "Alright, folks. I think we've absorbed enough genealogy for one day. Let's head home before we're mistaken for part of the exhibit."

No historical stop was complete without a gift shop, and Norma insisted on buying a postcard featuring a seventeenth-century map. "For inspiration," she claimed. Phil bought nothing, muttering about clutter, while Graham picked up a small book on Quebec's seigneurial system.

Back in the car, they settled into the familiar rhythm of road trip banter. The seats seemed harder than before, their limbs heavier. The thought of their own beds back in Percyville grew sweeter by the mile.

"You know," Phil said after a long silence, "I'm actually glad we stopped. Didn't learn a thing about myself, but it's humbling, in a way. All those names, all those lives. Reminds you you're just a speck on the timeline."

Norma smirked. "A speck with flat feet and sore hips."

"Exactly."

Graham smiled faintly, eyes on the road. "Funny thing about history. Even if it's not your family, you can still feel connected to it. Like stepping into someone else's shoes for a moment."

"Preferably shoes with better arch support," Norma quipped.

They laughed; the car filled with warmth despite their fatigue. Outside, the sun broke through the remaining clouds, painting the landscape gold. Home was still hours away, but they could already imagine the relief of familiar pillows and the luxury of sleeping in without alarm clocks or cobblestones.

Norma sighed, content despite herself. "Alright, gentlemen. Next trip, I vote we go somewhere with fewer hills, more chairs, and perhaps a genealogy archive that serves cocktails."

Phil perked up. "Now *that's* a history lesson I can get behind."

And with that, they drove on, three tired travelers carrying the echo of strangers' pasts, richer for the detour.

Chapter Eighteen

The air was damp with dew when Ellie and Quinn stepped out of the inn's side door, their shoes crunching softly on the gravel lane. The eastern sky was no more than a pale ribbon of light, and the world still carried the hush of night. Roosters stirred somewhere across the fields, their uncertain cries breaking the stillness.

They had said their goodbyes to Madame Rousseau the night before, but had found a cold breakfast of baguettes and cheese waiting for them on the table when they came down. Ellie tucked the bag of food away in her suitcase and they left their bag just inside the hall door.

Quinn pulled his coat tighter. "Early enough?"

Ellie smiled faintly, her breath visible in the chill. "It may be early here, but we'd normally have been up for hours." She huddled inside her coat and pulled the collar up. "But it *is* chilly."

They walked in silence along the narrow country road. The grass verges were wet, brushing against their shoes. A thin mist clung low to the ground, rising in ghostly sheets around the half-tilled fields. Quinn kept glancing toward the village steeple, a dark silhouette against the pale sky.

The cemetery appeared suddenly, a low wall of mossy stone set at the end of a dirt track. The wrought-iron gate hung slightly askew. Ellie touched it lightly, almost reverently, before pushing it open. This time she knew what she was looking for. Or who she was looking for.

Inside, the graveyard was quiet except for the soft drip of water from overgrown yews. The stones were uneven, leaning in different directions as if they had been pushed by time itself. Quinn let his hand trail along one of the lichen-covered crosses as they walked, then jammed it into his pocket to warm up.

They found the Ethier grave near the northern boundary, where the ground sloped gently downward toward a field. One simple marker stood, its inscription faint but legible in the growing light.

Ellie crouched down, brushing away moss with her gloved hand. She read aloud, voice low and steady:

"Anna Ethier, 1632 – 1663. A soul remembered."

"Gaston Ethier, 1657 – 1663. Lost to this world."

The words seemed to echo in the quiet, hanging in the mist.

Quinn knelt beside her, his knees resting on the damp earth. "Leonard must have been in such pain," he murmured. "Losing your whole family at once."

Ellie nodded, fingers lingering on the stone. "She would have been around thirty, and he only six years old."

For a long time, they said nothing. A blackbird sang hesitantly from a branch above, as though testing whether morning had truly come.

Ellie reached into her coat pocket and drew out a small clutch of wild flowers she had gathered on their way. She laid it gently across the stone.

"I don't know why I feel this," she whispered. "As if she's part of us. As if remembering her matters."

Quinn looked at her closely. The rising sun caught the edge of her dark hair, making it shine. "Maybe it's enough someone, three and a half centuries later, speaks her name again."

Ellie's throat tightened. She pressed her palm flat against the cold stone. "Anna. Gaston." The names drifted away like prayers into the pale morning air.

By the time they returned to the village road, the mist began to lift, revealing tiled rooftops and the smoke of early fires rising from chimneys.

The taxi they had arranged, a battered Peugeot driven by a man with a cap pulled low, was already waiting outside the inn.

The driver tipped his hat. "Limoges Gare?"

Quinn nodded. "Oui. Limoges." He gathered their bag and stashed it in the back of the taxi before settling into the backseat beside Ellie.

As the car jolted onto the road, Ellie turned in her seat to glance once more at the distant cemetery wall, now partly hidden behind hedgerows. For a fleeting moment she thought she saw the shimmer of white among the stones, as if someone stood there watching. She blinked, and the figure was gone. Her imagination would get the best of her one day.

The road wound through gentle hills, dotted with chestnut groves and stone farmhouses. Morning light spread across the countryside, gilding the tiled roofs, the slow-moving cows, the low bridges over narrow streams. Quinn rested his chin in his hand, gazing out the window.

"Strange, isn't it," he said finally, "how we chase stories backward through centuries, and somehow they reach forward to touch us."

Ellie settled deeper in the seat. "Stranger still, the touch feels so real."

The driver hummed softly to himself, an old folk tune, while the road unwound beneath them mile after mile.

***

At the Limoges train station, the great stone façade loomed with its green copper dome catching the sunlight. Travelers hurried in and out beneath the high clock. Quinn bought their tickets and they boarded a train headed north. Their compartment was nearly empty, save for an elderly couple murmuring quietly in the opposite corner. The train lurched, then gathered speed, sliding past the outskirts of Limoges and into the rolling countryside.

Ellie stared out the window, watching the fields recede. The rhythmic clatter of wheels against rails worked its way into her pulse, steady and almost hypnotic.

Quinn unwrapped the breakfast Madame Rousseau had left for them, and set out the bottles of water he had bought before boarding. He tore off a piece of the baguette and handed it to Ellie, nudging the parchment wrapped cheese her way. “By afternoon, we’ll be back in Paris.”

“Back where we began,” she said, before taking a bite of the delicious bread.

Hours passed. Villages flickered by, each with its steeple and cluster of red roofs. The train rattled across viaducts, skirted rivers, and plunged through tunnels. At times, Ellie closed her eyes and let the sway of the carriage rock her into a half-dream, where Anna and Gaston seemed to walk the corridors of time alongside her.

When at last the skyline of Paris appeared, the distant rise of towers, the sweep of the Seine, her heart quickened.

The taxi from Gare d’Austerlitz wove through familiar boulevards. Early afternoon sun struck the façades of Haussmann buildings, highlighting the iron balconies and tall windows. Ellie felt a rush of recognition as they pulled up before their hotel, the same modest place they had stayed in days earlier.

Inside, the lobby smelled faintly of polish and coffee. The concierge greeted them with a smile. “Ah, Monsieur, Madame, welcome back!”

Their room was as they remembered: cream walls, a king size bed with crisp linen, a tall window opening onto the street below where bicycles rattled past. Ellie breathed deeply, as though anchoring herself again in the city’s heartbeat.

***

They found a café two streets away, its awning striped red and white. The terrace tables were still half-filled with late lunch patrons; students with notebooks, business people lingering over wine, a family sharing platters of bread and cheese.

Ellie and Quinn chose a small table near the edge, ordering Quiche Lorraine, a salad, and two glasses of pale rosé. The food came quickly, fragrant with herbs.

Ellie broke off a piece of bread, dipping it in oil. "After the breakfast on the train, I thought I wouldn't be hungry. But Paris has a way of making you want to try everything in sight. At least once!"

Quinn raised his glass. "To Anna and Gaston," he said quietly.

Ellie clinked her glass against his. "To memory."

By mid-afternoon, they crossed the Pont au Double, the waters of the Seine glinting below. Notre Dame rose before them, its twin towers stark against the September sky. Even with the scars of fire and scaffolding that still clung to parts of the structure, it radiated solemn endurance.

Ellie paused at the square, her eyes traveling upward along the flying buttresses, the gargoyles, the tracery of stone.

Quinn stood beside her. "Centuries crumble, yet it stands. And those gargoyles are quite something."

"Have you considered creating something like that?" Ellie asked, hand shielding her eyes from the sun as she studied the creatures above. "Maybe carving them on bedposts," she grinned.

Quinn laughed. "You may joke, but I have been thinking about adding unique touches to some of my pieces. Gargoyles might work."

Inside, the vastness swallowed them. Sunlight filtered through stained glass, spilling jeweled colors across the floor. The quiet was shocking, filled only by the echo of footsteps and the faint murmur of prayer.

They wandered slowly down the nave, pausing at chapels, feeling the flicker of candle flames they passed as if they were embraces of calm.

At the south transept, Ellie stopped before the great rose window, its patterns of light spinning like a wheel of time. She thought of Anna's brief life, of Gaston's small hands clutching his mother's dress, of the fire that had taken them. And she thought, too, of how names, remembered, could shine like these windows through the centuries.

Quinn touched her arm gently. "Are you all right?"

Ellie nodded. "More than all right. I feel...connected."

They sat for a while in one of the wooden pews, the scent of incense lingering faintly. The afternoon light deepened toward gold. Tourists moved quietly, whispering. Somewhere a single note of an organ sounded, low and resonant, swelling into silence again. Everyone stopped, as if expecting to hear more, but nothing came.

When at last they stepped outside, the shadows of the towers stretched long across the square. The air had cooled, and the bells began to toll the hour, reverberating through the heart of Paris.

Ellie slipped her hand into Quinn's. He looked down at her, his expression unreadable but soft.

"No more chasing for today," he said. "Just Paris. Just now."

She nodded.

The bells of Notre Dame faded into the city's hum, leaving only the shimmer of twilight across the Seine. Ellie and Quinn lingered a while in the square, watching as the last golden light slid down the towers. The air was soft, the kind of September early evening that held the promise of autumn without yet letting go of summer.

Quinn glanced at her. "One more night in Paris. What shall we do with it?"

Ellie thought for a moment. "Something simple. Something that belongs to us, not to postcards."

He smiled. "Agreed. No Champs-Élysées, no grand restaurants. Just...Paris."

They walked hand in hand across the Pont Saint-Louis, the river glinting beneath them. The street lamps flickered to life, one by one, casting warm halos on the cobblestones. Musicians had already gathered on the bridge, an accordionist, a violinist, playing tunes that curled into the evening air. The music wasn't polished, but it carried a tenderness that felt like the city itself leaning close to whisper.

Ellie paused to listen, her hand tightening slightly around Quinn's. He studied her profile in the lamplight, the way her eyes softened, the way the music seemed to shape her silence.

"Shall we?" he asked, offering his other hand as though in invitation.

She laughed softly. "Here? In the street?"

"Why not?"

So they danced, hesitantly at first, then with growing ease, turning slowly on the stones as the violin spun its melancholy thread. The other passersby smiled but didn't intrude. For those few minutes, it was as though Paris had stopped to watch them, granting permission for two strangers to fold themselves into the city's rhythm.

When the song ended, Ellie leaned her head briefly against Quinn's shoulder. "That," she whispered, "is ours."

They wandered until they found a small bistro tucked on a side street; unpretentious, its windows fogged slightly from the warmth inside. The owner, a round man with kind eyes, welcomed them as if they were regulars.

The menu was handwritten on a chalkboard: duck with honey glaze, onion soup, a tarte aux pommes cooling on the counter. They ordered modestly, sharing dishes rather than each taking their own. A carafe of red wine stood between them, catching the candlelight.

As they ate, they spoke less of history and more of each other. Remembering their first meeting, Quinn's initial renting of the barn, the time Quinn ruined Ellie's favorite sweater in the wash, the quiet certainty they had felt on the day they decided to marry. Laughter came easily, but so did silences that felt full rather than empty.

At one point Ellie reached across the table and laid her hand across Quinn's. "I want you to know that you've given me something that I will never forget. Not just this trip, and finding out the why of my ancestor leaving. But you've given me a feeling of togetherness stronger than family. If that makes any sense? A feeling of safety and trust."

Quinn covered her hand with his. "I know exactly what you mean. We found each other when we needed to find and be found."

Ellie's eyes shone in the low light. "I didn't realize I'd married a poet."

"Just wait till you find out everything else about me over the next decades," he grinned.

"Promises, promises."

After dinner, they returned to the river. The night was deeper now, the Seine carrying black ripples touched by silver reflections of bridges and lamps. They walked slowly along the Quai de la Tournelle, away from the bustle, until they found a quiet spot where stone steps descended almost to the water's edge.

They sat there, shoulder to shoulder, the city stretching luminous around them. Boats passed occasionally, their low lights drifting like stars.

Ellie leaned against Quinn, resting her head where his chest rose and fell. "It doesn't feel like an ending," she murmured. "It feels like a beginning."

He kissed her hair. "That's what a good ending should feel like."

They stayed until the chill deepened, until their breaths rose in faint clouds. Above them, Notre Dame's towers loomed, guardians of memory and time. Around them, Paris carried on; lovers crossing bridges, laughter spilling from cafés, the eternal movement of the river.

Quinn finally stood, pulling Ellie up with him. "One last walk back to the hotel?"

She nodded, slipping her hand into the crook of his arm. They took two steps and her phone rang. "Who would be calling me here, now?" She pulled it out and read the text. "It's from Claudette. She wants to know if we could drop by tomorrow morning." Ellie raised an eyebrow to Quinn. "In lieu of more sightseeing? Because we have lunch with Gillian at noon, and our plane leaves at 4:30".

"I'm game if you are," Quinn said. "She's an interesting woman. I hope one day I'll get to read her memoir. I'm sure she has a lot of amazing stories to tell."

Ellie typed out a quick reply, read the response, and then tucked her phone away. "She'd like us to be there for ten thirty."

Quinn held out his arm once again, and together they walked through the winding streets, not hurried, not speaking much, letting Paris write itself quietly into the fabric of their last night.

Chapter Nineteen

The mid-morning sun was pouring into Graham's kitchen when Norma arrived, a brisk knock followed by the swish of the front door. She came in balancing a basket.

"Morning, Graham. I've brought you some cheese scones from Maggie. They'll go dry if you don't eat them soon." She set the basket down, dusting her hands against her coat.

Graham stood from his desk, looking pale but electric, as though he'd swallowed a light bulb. "They're in," he said breathlessly.

Norma blinked. "The scones? Yes, they're right there."

"No! My DNA results. They came in this morning."

"Oh!" She widened her eyes, instantly intrigued. "Already? Good heavens, I thought you said it would take weeks yet."

"So did I, but, well, I checked this morning and there it was. Right at the top." His voice dropped to a whisper. "A match."

Norma tilted her head, amused. "You look like you've seen a ghost. Who's popped up then? A Viking raider? A Russian countess?"

Graham waved his hand. "Not nearly so romantic. A man named Henri Tremblay."

Norma paused, her brows knitting. "A relative of Lucien, do you think?"

"Possibly." Graham said the word with some difficulty, like a child tasting a new food. "I'm still not sure, but there it is, plain as day. I've been staring at it for hours."

"Well then," Norma said cheerfully, "we'd better have a look together. Where's the machine?"

Graham's computer hummed on the small desk against the wall, the Ancestry site open. He pointed at the screen as if Norma might miss it. "There. Do you see? Henri. Now, what do we do?"

Norma leaned over his shoulder. "Well then. That seems quite straightforward, doesn't it? But..." she pulled out her phone and dialed. "Phil? We need your help. Graham's DNA results are in and there's someone named Henri Tremblay and..." She stopped talking and nodded. "I'll time you." She turned to Graham. "He'll be here in five minutes." She pushed the sleeve of her sweater up and studied her watch.

"You're really timing him?" Graham asked with a chuckle.

The minutes passed. She held up a finger. A car door slammed. Norma gave Graham a wink. Before Graham could answer, the doorbell rang.

Phil arrived with the briskness of someone who enjoyed being called in for emergencies. Being a recent technology learner, especially where genealogy was concerned, he was always eager and ready to troubleshoot.

"What's all the fuss?" he said, dropping his coat onto a chair. "Let's see the DNA results."

Graham gestured helplessly at the computer. "I've been matched. To Henri Tremblay. How can we be sure he's related to Lucien?"

Phil leaned in, squinting at the screen. "Well, would you look at that. What we'll do now is access this Henri's family tree, if it's public."

"Oh, goodness," Norma moaned, "don't let it be private." She held up crossed fingers and closed her eyes.

Graham stood up and gave Phil his seat at the computer, then pulled two more chairs around for himself and Norma.

Phil hit a few keys. "It's public."

Norma and Graham let out held breaths and stared at the screen as Henri's tree appeared.

"His father is Paul," Graham said. He fumbled on the desk for a pad of paper where he had made his notes. His fingers skimmed along the page and stopped. "From what Armand said in Baie-Saint-Paul, he believed that was Lucien's youngest son."

"Let's be sure," Phil murmured, clicking on Paul's name and bringing *his* family group up on screen.

"There, there," Norma pointed to Paul's father's name. "Lucien! It's him!"

"Wait, let's see who Lucien's parents are," Phil said. Bringing up Lucien's family showed that his mother was Emilie Tremblay, no father noted. "I'd say that's a solid match. Congratulations, Graham."

"Congratulations?" Graham muttered, eyes blinking as if caught in headlights, a bit stunned. "Now what am I supposed to do?"

"You write to him," Phil said matter-of-factly.

"Write? As in an email?"

"As in a message right here on Ancestry. That's what it's for. People expect it."

Norma nodded firmly. "Of course. Henri wouldn't be on there if he didn't want to be contacted. He's Lucien's grandson, so, he might even be thrilled to hear from you."

"Or horrified," Graham said darkly. "Imagine opening your inbox to discover a stranger claiming to be family."

"Not strange," Norma corrected. "Distinguished. Respectable. Nervous, perhaps, but that only adds charm."

Phil clapped his hands together. "Right. Let's draft this message. See this little box with a picture in the upper left, beside the words Tremblay Family Tree? That's the owner of this tree. In this case, it's Henri." He clicked Henri's name. "And this is where we send a message." The cursor blinked, patient and merciless. "There you are," he said. "Now just say hello."

Graham swallowed. "Hello?"

"Yes. Simple as that. *Hello, Henri.*"

Graham switched places with Phil, hands hovering above the keyboard like frightened birds. "I can't just write *hello.* That sounds... empty. Unimaginative. What if he thinks I'm rude?"

Norma leaned over. "Then say *Dear Henri.* It's polite, but not too stiff."

Graham typed it in. *Dear Henri,* "There," he said. "Done. Next line." He hesitated. "What do I even say? I don't know him. I don't know if he wants to know me."

"You acknowledge the match," Norma said. "That's all. Something like: 'I see we've been matched as relatives through Lucien.'"

Graham tapped the keys, reading as he typed. "*I recently received my results and noticed that we're related through Lucien.*" He wrung his hands. "Doesn't that sound... abrupt?"

"No," Norma said. "It sounds honest."

Phil gave Graham a look. "You're overthinking this. Keep going. Tell him you'd like to connect."

Graham took a deep breath. "All right. '*As I am new to this, I would be very glad to hear from you, if you're willing.*'"

Norma beamed. "Lovely. Friendly, respectful, and not too long. Perfect."

But Graham frowned. "What if it's *too* short? What if he thinks I'm uninterested?"

Phil groaned good-naturedly. "Then add one more sentence. Something like: '*I'd like to learn a little more about the Tremblay side of the family, when convenient.*' That shows curiosity."

Graham typed again.

They all leaned back and Norma read the message aloud:

Dear Henri,

I recently received my DNA results on Ancestry and noticed that we're related through Lucien. As I am new to this, I would be very glad to hear from you, if you're willing. I'd also like to learn a little more about the Tremblay side of the family, when convenient.

With best regards,
Dr. Graham Brody

"There," Phil said. "Simple, clear, polite."

"It's not too much?" Graham asked.

"It's just right," Norma assured him. "Like butter on toast. Enough to cover, not enough to drip."

"Wait!" Phil said. Everyone froze.

"What? What?" Graham asked, wide-eyed.

"Let's add the picture you have of Lucien at the farmhouse," Phil suggested. He held out his hand and Graham passed it to him. Phil took a picture of it with his phone, loaded it to Graham's family tree, then added it to the message to Henri. "There. Done."

Graham stared at the screen, his finger hovering over the mouse. "Once I send this, there's no taking it back."

"That's the point," Phil said.

"What if he doesn't reply?"

"Then you'll know you tried," Norma said gently.

"What if he *does* reply?"

Phil grinned. "Then you'll have a new cousin."

Graham rubbed his temples. "You make it sound so easy."

"It *is* easy," Norma said. "It's the waiting that's hard. But you'll manage. We'll manage. Now go on, press send."

Graham's hand trembled slightly. He adjusted his glasses, shifted in his chair, took a breath, let it out, and muttered, "All right. Here goes nothing."

He clicked.

The message whooshed away, leaving the screen blank and his heart thudding.

For a long moment, no one spoke. The three of them simply watched the screen, as though expecting Henri to materialize instantly with a warm reply.

When nothing happened, Graham sagged back in his chair. "That's it? It's gone?"

"That's it," Phil confirmed. "Congratulations, Graham. You've officially reached out."

Norma squeezed his shoulder. "You've done something brave today. Whatever comes of it, you'll never regret trying."

Graham let out a shaky laugh. "I feel as though I've just leapt off a cliff."

"Yes," Norma said with a twinkle. "But you've leapt into family. There are worse places to land."

Phil stretched and stood. "Now comes the waiting game. Check your messages tomorrow, and the day after. You never know, Henri might be just as eager to hear from you."

Graham nodded slowly, still dazed. "Henri Tremblay. Grandson of Lucien. And here I am, writing to him. Who would have thought?"

"Life's full of surprises," Norma said, lifting the basket of scones and setting one on a plate. "Now eat this before it goes cold. You'll need your strength."

Despite his nerves, Graham found himself smiling.

Chapter Twenty

Ellie and Quinn had slept in on their last morning in Paris. Check out time was eleven, but their meeting with Claudette was for ten thirty. Quinn ordered a full room service breakfast for them and they ate in bed, watching the rain against the windows.

The weather cleared by the time they checked out and reached the familiar apartment building near the Opera Garnier. The vines draping over the stone façade glistened in the gray light, and Ellie felt a quiet comfort in recognizing the steps, the carved door, the little brass plate with Claudette's name on it. She wasn't nervous this time. The nerves belonged to their first visit, the one where introductions and polite smiles carried the air. Today felt different; like returning to an aunt or cousin you'd grown to like after that first shy dinner.

Quinn tapped lightly on the door. Almost immediately, the sound of wheels hummed against the floorboards inside. The door swung open to reveal Claudette, perched in her wheelchair, a knitted shawl over her rounded shoulders. Her eyes, still sharp, still mischievous, lit up when she saw them.

"Ah, mes petits Canadiens," she said, her voice warm with obvious delight on seeing them again. "Thank you for coming back."

Ellie bent down to kiss her cheeks. "It's our pleasure."

"Bon," Claudette replied. "The first time, it is always *les politesses*. Too much sugar, not enough salt. But the second time... is when we talk like real people." She winked, and her whole face seemed to glow with it.

Quinn laughed, holding the door wider so Claudette could wheel back into the apartment. The space looked just as Ellie remembered: velvet curtains, worn but luxurious; books stacked in unruly towers; photographs half-hidden among knick-knacks; sketches and fabric swatches pinned to cork boards like butterflies. Today the assistants were absent, the workroom quiet.

"Simone is in the back with her sewing machine," Claudette said as she maneuvered herself toward the armchair near the window. "The girl never stops. I swear she even dreams with a needle in hand."

Ellie and Quinn settled on the sofa, familiar now, the cushions sinking just right. Claudette parked herself near them, her fingers tapping the wooden armrest of her chair as if keeping time to a silent tune.

"There is something I want you to take to Norma," she said, her gaze steady on Ellie. Claudette's tone became quieter, as though she had waited for this second meeting to say what she hadn't the first.

Ellie leaned forward. "Something for my aunt?"

"Yes." Claudette's voice softened, her accent curling around the words like smoke. She held out a small package and handed it to Ellie. "It is just for Norma." She tilted her head, eyes twinkling but firm. "Do you promise to put it directly in her hands?"

Ellie took the parcel and nodded. "I promise." She made a show of placing it in the inside pocket of her purse and closing it up.

"Good." Claudette let out a breath and, for a moment, seemed smaller in her chair. But she straightened quickly, wheeling herself a little closer. "Norma and I, we go back to when the world was very different. We shared laughter, but also... how do I put it..." She paused, weighing the words. "We shared loss."

Quinn glanced at Ellie. Claudette's face, usually lively, had taken on a reflective stillness.

"When we were young," Claudette continued, "we both carried children who never came to be. Miscarriages. Such an ugly word. As though we had misplaced them, like keys or scarves." Her voice faltered just enough to betray the decades-old wound beneath. "But no. We did not mis-carry. We carried them in our hearts, and then lost them."

Ellie felt the words land heavy in her chest. She thought of Aunt Norma, her matter-of-fact strength, never hinting at this secret history.

"She never told me," Ellie said quietly.

"She would not." Claudette's eyes softened. "Your aunt always buttoned her sorrow tight, like a coat. I… I screamed. I cursed. I threw things at the wall. Norma… she folded it all inside. And though she moved on, you must know such things leave their mark."

Quinn reached over, letting his hand rest lightly on Ellie's knee. Neither spoke, but the gesture was enough to tell her he was thinking of Ellie's own loss of her first husband and daughter.

Claudette sighed, then added, "I tell you this not to make you sad. But so you know the truth; that your aunt's silences are as full as her words. And yes, maybe I have no right to tell you this at all. But I love Norma, and sometimes other people understanding events that shaped you makes life a bit easier. You don't have to tell her you know, or even speak of it to her."

Just then, the hum of the sewing machine stopped, and footsteps padded into the room. Simone appeared, her arms full of fabric, her expression bright. She looked as polished as their first visit; hair brushed sleek, lipstick bold. Her energy was the same: vibrant, restless, like a spark that refused to die.

"Ellie!" Simone set the fabric down with a flourish. "I've been waiting for you."

Ellie rose, smiling. "For me?"

"Yes. For two days I've been working." Simone darted into the hallway and returned with a box wrapped in tissue. She held it out like an offering. "Open it."

Ellie obeyed, unwrapping the delicate paper to reveal a blouse in the softest blue fabric that shimmered faintly in the lamplight. It was elegant but practical, structured yet fluid.

"I made it for you," Simone declared, her pride obvious. "I knew your shape the moment I saw you. I did not need to measure. I see these things."

Quinn let out a low whistle. "That's... beautiful."

"Come, come," Simone pulled her by the hand towards a door across the room. "Go in there and try it on."

Ellie returned minutes later. The blouse fell perfectly, neither tight nor loose, as though Simone had sculpted it around her body without even touching her. She turned toward the mirror. For a moment, she hardly recognized herself.

"It fits," Simone said simply, satisfaction glowing in her smile. "See? I told you."

Ellie turned back, touched almost to tears. "It's incredible. Truly. I've never had anything fit me this well. Thank you."

"You give me joy by loving it," Simone replied. "That is all I want."

Claudette chuckled. "The girl has an eye. If only the world would open its eyes to her."

For a while, they sat in the warm glow of the fire, Simone talking about her dreams of Milan, Quinn cracking jokes about Parisian pigeons, Claudette chiming in with sharp little quips that kept them laughing. The heaviness of Claudette's earlier confession didn't vanish, but it wove itself into the atmosphere; like an undercurrent, shaping the river without showing on the surface.

Eventually, Ellie glanced at the clock and stood, Quinn following. "We should be going. We have a lunch date with my aunt before we catch our plane home."

Claudette wheeled closer, then, with a small grunt, pushed herself up to stand. She wrapped Ellie in a hug, pressing her close. Her arms were strong despite her size, her cheek warm against Ellie's.

"Take care of Norma," Claudette whispered against her ear. "And take care of yourself. Families are not perfect. They wound each other, they hide truths, they lose and they break. But still, they are the roots. Without them, we drift like leaves in the river, no place to land. Remember this."

Ellie held her tighter. "I will."

When Claudette finally let go, Simone kissed Ellie's cheeks, whispering, "Wear the blouse when you need courage."

Quinn helped Ellie into her coat, and together they said their good-byes. The stairwell echoed with their voices as they descended, and as Ellie stepped back into the cool Paris air, the blouse against her skin and Claudette's words in her heart, she knew the visit had given her something she couldn't quite name; a piece of her family's hidden past, and a glimpse of the ties that bound them, fragile and unbreakable all at once.

Chapter Twenty-One

Ellie and Quinn left Claudette's building to find the cobbled street outside gleaming faintly from another shower. Paris carried its usual perfume of roasted chestnuts, exhaust, and possibility. Claudette's hug lingered in Ellie's bones, warm and grounding, but her words, about families as roots and about the silences Norma carried, kept circling in her head.

Quinn shifted his bag on his shoulder and nudged Ellie. "You ready?"

Ellie nodded. "Yeah. Gillian said she'd already be at the restaurant. She's not one for being late, apparently."

"Runs in the blood?" Quinn teased.

Ellie smirked. "Not in mine."

They flagged down a taxi, and the driver helped them wedge their rolling suitcases into the trunk. As the car wound through Paris traffic toward Saint-Germain, Ellie tapped her fingers nervously against her knee. Gillian was still new in her life, a surprise discovery that had turned the family tree into something more like a bramble, tangled and spreading. They'd met once in Liverpool, awkward and cautious, like two puzzle pieces trying to see if their edges matched. Then more linked and solid when Gillian had flown to Quebec for Ellie and Quinn's marriage. But right from the start, there had been a spark; a recognition, despite the years and the distance, something connected them.

The taxi pulled up outside a narrow-fronted restaurant with striped awnings and polished brass handles. The name, *Le Jardin Intérieur,* was etched in gold letters above the door.

"Looks nice," Quinn said, eyeing the menu posted outside.

"Nice enough that our luggage might be a problem," Ellie muttered.

But once inside, the host, after a brief lift of his eyebrows, ushered them to a booth along the wall where the high leather back offered both privacy and space to slide their bags discreetly underneath. Ellie breathed a sigh of relief.

Gillian was already there, a glass of sparkling water in front of her. She waved with a grin, transforming her face, bright with energy.

"Ellie!" Gillian said, standing quickly. She was about five inches taller than Ellie's five foot nothing, and she was slim. Her bob-cut dark hair bounced as she moved and her wire-rimmed glasses highlighted her blue eyes. At the moment, those eyes crinkled at the corners when she smiled. "And Quinn. It's lovely to see you both again."

They exchanged quick hugs, and Ellie slid into the booth opposite her aunt, marveling again at the strangeness of calling someone just two years older *aunt.* Seeing her mother's face in Gillian's always made her heart skip.

"You look amazing," Ellie said honestly. Gillian wore a fitted blue blazer with matching pants, and a white blouse, smart but not stiff.

"Thank you. But you have to, don't you?" Gillian smirked, her Liverpool accent lilting. "Running a cleaning business, everyone expects you to look like the help, but I believe you should dress like the boss to be treated like the boss. It's paid off."

Quinn looked at the menu as he spoke. "And how is business these days?"

"Oh, it's flying," Gillian said, leaning forward, clearly proud. "Like I told you, I started with just me and a mop five years ago. Last month I hired a dozen new people and now I've got thirty employees, contracts with offices, hotels, even the university. Liverpool's a dirty city, but that's good for me." She laughed, the sound infectious.

Ellie grinned, warmed by her confidence. "That's incredible. Honestly, I can barely keep my house clean."

"Then you'd never last with me," Gillian teased. "I run a tight ship. But let's not talk about mops." She lowered her voice slightly, conspiratorial. "I've got something to show you. Well, to tell you. About my Mum's side."

Ellie loved Gillian's enthusiasm. "Do tell."

"Kay's been teaching me how to dig," Gillian said, eyes glittering with excitement. "She's brilliant, that one. You should see her with online records; it's like watching a detective. She sat me down and introduced me to Ancestry and other sites; showed me parish registers, census returns, and all that. I didn't know where to start, but she walked me through. Birth certificates, death certificates, marriage lines; you can trace the whole web if you know how to read them." She picked up her menu then slapped it back on the table, startling them all. "And she said she'll take me down to the records office one day soon, too. Teach me how to use the microfilm machines. How interesting is that?"

"There's nothing like feeding your first reel into the machine," Ellie agreed, grinning at her aunt's excitement.

Quinn sipped his water, listening intently.

"But the big record for me," Gillian continued, "was the 1911 census. Kay showed me how to search it online. My Mum's grandfather turns up in Toxteth, working as a dock laborer. But here's the thing: the census lists the number of children born to the marriage. And it showed three that died young. Mum says no one ever spoke about that. It was hidden history, but it was actually right there in black and white."

Ellie blinked, the words resonating after what Claudette had shared only an hour before. Children lost, grief folded into silence.

The waiter arrived, interrupting their reverie with a basket of bread. They ordered; Ellie a salade niçoise, Quinn a steak-frites, Gillian moules marinières, and when the waiter left, the conversation picked up again, urgent and buzzing.

"That was often the case," Ellie murmured. "I had an older client who only found out he had two sisters in the very same way. It's heartbreaking."

"It is," Gillian agreed. "But then Kay dug further. Ship manifests. Turns out, one of Mum's cousins emigrated to Canada in the 1920s. Quebec, to be exact. There's a record of him on the *SS Montcalm*, leaving Liverpool, age twenty-one, a carpenter. Can you believe that? I've got family your side of the ocean, Ellie. Maybe even still there."

Ellie's breath caught. "In Quebec? Really?"

"Really." Gillian's grin widened. "Kay showed me how to use Canadian records, and we found out he married there, and had at least two kids. Names are a bit fuzzy at the moment, but Kay's got a knack for piecing it together. She says we should try to track the descendants, see if they're still around. Imagine that; more family I never knew about, and maybe not far from you at all. Mom is even more excited than I am."

Ellie's mind spun. Family scattered like seeds, crossing oceans, leaving traces in ink and paper. It was one thing to know in theory people emigrated, another to see the line on a ship manifest and realize it was *her* blood who had boarded that ship.

Quinn leaned in, intrigued. "So Kay taught you all this, about how to use records?"

"Oh yes," Gillian said, animated. "Census returns, parish registers for baptisms and burials, probate records; wills can be goldmines, you know. And the shipping lists. She even showed me maps of old streets, so you can see where they lived, what the houses might have looked like, if they're still there. It's like peeling back wallpaper in an old house layer by layer, you see what was underneath."

Gillian's voice brimmed with pride as she talked about her late nights poring over records, the thrill of finding a name repeated, of realizing the person on an old register was *hers.*

"It makes you see your own life differently," she said. "I built my cleaning business, yeah, but those dockers, those carpenters, amongst many others, they built the bones of the city. Ordinary people, but they carried us here. Makes me want to do more, somehow."

Ellie nodded, touched. "I know exactly what you mean."

Lunch arrived, steaming and fragrant, and for a few minutes they ate in contented silence, the clink of cutlery and the murmur of French conversation filling the air. Between bites Ellie filled Gillian in on what they had found out in about her Ethier family, and Gillian peppered her with questions. She got so excited at one point that she kicked one of their suitcases. "I'm so sorry," she said. Their luggage sat tucked beneath the booth, out of sight but ever-present, a reminder of the clock ticking toward departure.

Halfway through, a hostess approached, frowning slightly. "Excusez-moi, mesdames... are these bags yours?" She gestured to the neatly stowed suitcases.

"Yes," Ellie said quickly, heart thudding. "We're flying home this afternoon."

The hostess pursed her lips but, after a moment, nodded. "D'accord. Please keep them out of the walkway."

"They are," Gillian replied, smiling disarmingly but with a steeliness that registered with the hostess. She retreated, mollified.

Ellie exhaled. "That was close."

"Always a problem, luggage," Gillian said cheerfully, spooning broth from her mussels. "But we made it work. Story of our family, right?"

The words struck Ellie; an offhand joke, but true. Always making it work, with whatever they carried.

By the time dessert was offered, Gillian glanced at her watch. "Nearly two. You'd better head out. Don't want to miss your flight."

Reluctantly, Ellie nodded. "You're right."

They signaled for the bill, which Gillian insisted on covering. "Don't argue," she said firmly. "Next time you're in Liverpool, you can treat me. But this one's mine."

They gathered their bags, sliding them out from under the booth, and stood in the small space of the restaurant's aisle. Gillian hugged Ellie first, tight and fierce.

"I'm glad we found each other," she said. "Really glad."

"Me too," Ellie whispered.

Then Gillian hugged Quinn, laughing. "You keep her steady, okay? She looks like she could drift off chasing history otherwise."

"I'll do my best," Quinn promised.

At the door, sunlight broke briefly through the clouds, casting the street in gold. The three of them stood together one last moment before Ellie and Quinn hailed a taxi for the airport. Gillian waved until they were out of sight.

Inside the cab, Ellie gazed out the window, the city sliding past. She thought of Claudette's hug, of Gillian's discoveries, of roots and branches stretching across oceans. Families were messy, complicated, full of silences and secrets; but these were hers. And that, she realized, was enough.

Chapter Twenty-Two

Graham sat in a stream of early morning sun at his kitchen table, coffee at hand. The tiny house was still and quiet. A soft knock at the door disturbed his calm, but he smiled as Norma's face peered through the glass. He waved her in.

Norma dumped a packet of letters on the table and took a Cozy Corner Café pastry bag to the kitchen. "Sara said the postman wasn't sure what to do with your mail, so she set him straight and took this in. You should be up and running with a key to your mailbox tomorrow."

"Thanks for that, Norma. Much appreciated." He sorted through the flyers and envelopes; nothing urgently required his attention so he pushed them into a corner of the table.

Norma found a couple of plates, placed a chocolate croissant on each, nudging one toward him, the other for herself. "There." She grinned at him as she sat beside him. "Now we can get on with the important matter."

Graham frowned as he pulled apart the pastry. "And what might that be?" He popped a piece in his mouth and marveled at the skill his granddaughter had with baking.

"Remember when Maggie helped you set up your Ancestry account when you moved in?"

He nodded, mouth full of another portion.

"Well, she knew you'd need help, so she added it to my tablet so you wouldn't miss anything important, at least until you get sorted, and then I'll delete it."

"Really?" Raised eyebrows.

She held up a hand. "Only until I show you what you need to do. Then I'm deleting my email address. Not to worry."

"Much appreciated. I never thought moving and getting settled would be so... exhausting."

Norma brushed the crumbs from her fingers and wiped them on a napkin before placing her tablet on the table. "So, do you want to see the message from Henri or not? I haven't opened it, because it's not mine to read, but I know it arrived."

"He responded already?" Graham wiped his hands and took the tablet in shaking hands. He opened the message and started to read.

"Oh, for pity's sake!" Norma exclaimed. "Out loud, please."

He winced. "Sorry. So, the subject is Re: Lucien." He glanced up at her. "Why am I so nervous about this?"

Norma patted his arm and motioned him to continue.

Dear Dr. Brody,

Thank you for your message. It came as a surprise, to say the least, but not an unwelcome one. I am a sociology student getting my masters, and my current project is the genealogy of families. I'm using my own family and have been searching for answers about my grandfather Lucien, to no avail. Until now. Relatives I spoke with never knew who his father was. We assumed the man was a secret the family wanted buried.

I never knew my grandfather, as he died when I was young, but my father said he was a kind, generous man, to everyone. The photograph you included... it's him. The farmhouse is where I spent summers as a child. That's where he was raised by his mother Emilie's parents.

I've never heard your family name mentioned, but after reading your message, I went to Ancestry and saw the DNA connection. I'm going to assume you are connected to Lucien's father. At least, I hope that's who you are. And strangely, it feels like a missing piece settling into place.

I would very much like to speak with you. I can come to Percyville this afternoon, if that suits you. (Can you tell I'm excited?) I will bring what I have found, photos, stories, papers. Maybe together we can make sense of the silences our families left us.

Warmly,

Henri Tremblay

Graham read the email twice, then slowly lowered the tablet. He didn't say anything right away. Just nodded, his eyes wet.

Norma murmured, "He's coming, can you imagine that?"

Graham nodded. "Yes. And he's bringing the rest of the story with him."

"We have to tell everyone." Norma stood, as if to dash off that very moment and gather the Heritage Harvesters.

"Wait!" Graham took her arm and eased her back into her seat. "Wait," he said more quietly. "I want to meet with him first, if you don't mind. Get my thoughts in order before I share anything more."

"Of course," Norma nodded her understanding. "And you have to send Henri another message."

"What?"

Norma shook her head and smiled. "You have to give him directions, and put the poor boy out of his misery. Tell him yes, your grandfather was Lucien's father. Then you can share the details of what you both know when he gets here."

"Will you be here when he comes?" Graham asked. He didn't look at her, afraid she'd refuse.

"If that's what you want, I'd be delighted to join you." Her words were soft but strong, assuring him he was not alone in this.

Graham took a deep breath. "Tearing down brick walls is an exhausting business."

"It is," Norma agreed. "And then after you respond to him, we'll go for a walk around the lake and into the forest."

"Just what I need," he grumbled. "More exercise." But within minutes his message had been sent, his shoes were on, and they were out the door into the fresh air and sunshine.

***

Graham stood by the front window of his tiny house, hands in his pockets. He'd been watching the road for the past twenty minutes; not anxiously, but with the calm anticipation of someone waiting for a pleasant surprise. Henri said he'd be there around three and it was now ten minutes to.

The temperatures were mild, with puffy clouds and energetic birds dashing amongst the trees outside. A kettle boiled gently on the stove, and the fresh air wafted in through the open windows.

A small grey car pulled into the gravel lot, and a man in his thirties stepped out. He was tall, with a shock of brilliant red hair, and wore a pair of round wire rim glasses he pushed up his nose as he looked around. His face was soft around sharp, intelligent eyes, and his gaze suggested he'd read a lot of books and waited for a lot of answers.

He carried a tote bag and a manila folder. No dramatics. Just a quiet arrival.

Graham opened the door before he knocked, his hand outstretched and a warm smile on his face. "You must be Henri."

Henri grinned, taking the offered hand. "And you must be Graham." He pointed at his hair and then at Graham's, though Graham's was a fading red with more grey. "If I had any doubts, I don't anymore."

Graham stepped back and ushered Henri inside. The younger man stopped on the threshold, taking in the atmosphere. "This is great. I've never been inside a tiny house before. It's bigger than it looks. And it smells like cedar and... old books."

"Probably a bit of both. Come in. Tea's on."

"Wait, wait," gasped a voice from outside the screen door. Both men turned to see Norma fling open the door and hurry inside. "I'm sorry I'm late. I had to jiggle something in the car engine, and it was being petty about it."

Henri's eyebrow raised and he hid a smile as Norma stepped forward and held out a hand. "You must be Henri. We're so pleased to find you. I'm Norma, a good friend of Graham, and member of the Heritage Harvesters."

"Nice to meet you," Henri said. "Who are the Heritage Harvesters?"

Graham brought the teapot to the already set up table and motioned for them to take a seat. "Let's have a cup of tea and one of my granddaughter's cookies." He pushed a plate of assorted cookies towards Henri and watched his eyes light up.

"Maggie owns the Cozy Corner Café," Norma explained. "You probably passed it on the highway."

Henri nodded, covering his mouth as he chewed. "I did. The parking lot was packed."

"She's an amazing baker," Graham said, obvious pride radiating through him.

"The Heritage Harvesters meet there every week," Norma said as she dropped three sugar cubes into her tea, avoiding Graham's frown at her high sugar consumption. "We're a group of seniors who are learning to write our memoirs."

"Maggie's best friend, Ellie, is teaching us," Graham added.

"We often come across family mysteries to solve." Norma waved her spoon in Henri's direction. "And we solve them, if we can."

"That's fascinating," Henri said, his grin seeming plastered on his face. He took another bite and took a deeper look around the tiny house. "Do all you Heritage Harvesters live in tiny homes?"

Norma snorted. "Almost. Phil is about to move in, Tess prefers the retirement home, especially after recently losing her husband. Shirley, her sister Ruth, and Ruth's husband, Jeremy, all live in the largest of the homes here in the community. I'm still wandering the halls of the home I raised my children in."

"Are you thinking of coming here too?" Henri asked.

Norma hesitated. "I have so much stuff," she mumbled.

"You know we'd all help you," Graham said. "You should talk to Sara. It would be fun having everyone close together."

"I'll think about it," she said quickly before turning to Henri. "So, Henri. Tell us a bit about yourself."

"Well," he said, wiping his fingers and reaching for his folder. "As I mentioned, I'm at university studying for my masters in sociology, and I wanted something unique for my final project. I want to focus on family units when I graduate, and I thought knowing how my own family was formed would be an interesting topic."

"I bet you didn't expect this," Norma said.

Henri sat back and shook his head. "You're right about that. As I started asking the family questions, the more I became aware of the gaping hole of who Lucien's father was."

"And no one had any clues?" Graham asked.

"None." He opened the manila folder and slid a photo across the table.

It was Lucien, older now; maybe in his forties. He had kind eyes. A narrow face. A hint of a smile, as if someone had caught him mid-thought.

"That's Lucien. My grandfather. I've only ever seen maybe five photos of him. He didn't like the camera."

Graham studied it, then nodded slowly. "He looks... kind." He handed Henri a picture of his own father, Duncan, that lay on the table between them. "That same mouth as my father. The tilt of the head. You see it?"

Henri nodded. "I do. I never knew what we were missing before. Now I see it everywhere. There are two other red heads in my family, but no one alive knows where it came from." He pulled out another paper; Lucien's baptismal certificate. It listed his mother, Emilie Tremblay. The space for his father's name was blank. "Have you seen this?"

Norma nodded. "We have."

"And we have something to show you," Graham said. He pulled Emilie's original letters from the envelope and handed them to Henri.

Henri took a minute to read them in French, then read them once again. "Wow. How did you get these?"

Graham shook his head. "They were in a box of my father's possessions. I don't know if he received them from his father, or someone else. That part is a mystery."

"But this Stuart Brody never came looking for Lucien," Henri said quietly.

"Which leads us to believe he never even knew about Lucien," Norma said.

Graham took a deep breath. "My grandfather was a good man. I doubt he would have left Lucien on his own, even with his grandparents, if he'd known he had a son."

They sat in silence for a moment, sipping tea. It wasn't awkward. It was reverent.

"But like I said," Graham continued, "I don't know how my father got them. It seems he hadn't read them. The envelope was still sealed when I got them. It was like they were tossed into his box and forgotten."

"Some mysteries are not meant to be solved," Henri said, reaching for another cookie. "But I believe that things happen for a reason, no matter how unbelievable."

Norma shrugged. "There are more things in heaven and earth, Horatio, than are dreamt of in your philosophy."

Graham grinned. "I didn't know you read Shakespeare, Norma."

"There's a lot you don't know about me."

Henri shifted in his seat. "I just want to thank you again for writing. Most people wouldn't. Most people don't want to look backward."

"I didn't, either," Graham admitted. "Until the past came unboxed with my books and socks."

That made him smile.

"What do *you* know about Lucien?" Norma asked.

"I was told he was a quiet man, steady. But there was a part of him that never quite sat still. Like he was waiting for something. Maybe it was this. Maybe he never thought it would come."

Graham nodded. "It came. Just a bit late. But maybe not too late."

"My dad said he was a good father, more involved with the family than most men in those days."

Graham reached into a small drawer and pulled out the photo of Lucien as a child, the one in front of the farmhouse. He slid it to Henri. "That's the one I found. Started all of this. It belongs with you. And I've made copies of these as well." Graham handed him the documents they had accumulated in their search, birth records, death records, and even a copy of the map of the seigneurial plot in Baie-Saint-Paul.

Henri took everything and focused on the photo. "Thank you. It's the youngest I've ever seen him."

He looked around the tiny house, then back at Graham. "Do you mind if I take a picture? Just... for the family tree?"

He smiled. "Of me, or the house?"

"Both," he said, lifting his phone.

***

Henri lingered in the tiny house longer than he had intended. The clock above the sink indicated the passing hours, yet neither he nor Graham seemed in any hurry to end the conversation.

They spent the last stretch speaking not only of ancestors long gone, but of the lives still unfolding; their parents and siblings, nieces and nephews, the quirks of aunts who still sent letters on thick stationery. Graham, with his deliberate, almost judicial way of speaking, had described the clan stretched across New Brunswick from origins in Scotland. Henri, leaning forward with his hands clasped, painted a picture of the Montreal kin: boisterous cousins who argued loudly in French over holiday meals, uncles who played fiddles until dawn, and a grandmother who could silence the whole table with a single look.

What struck Graham most was the similarities that lay beneath the surface differences. Both families, English and French, had scattered over borders and oceans, yet their stories were held together by the same threads; love of land, loyalty to kin, the stubborn determination to survive.

Henri looked at the picture of his grandfather on the family farm again. "We spent a lot of good times at this farm." He looked up at Graham with a smile. "Last year I bought the deed from the family. Everyone can still come visit, but my wife and I want to move there. She can work remotely, and we want to start *our* family in the Tremblay farmhouse."

"We went there, "Graham told him. "We visited the farm, met some neighbours."

"Peeked in a window," Norma winked. "It's a beautiful place."

"It needs a bit of work," Henri admitted, "but I'm pretty good with a hammer."

Norma held up a hand, a frown on her face. "I do have one question though." The men turned to her. "Why wasn't Emilie buried with her parents? Or her parents with her, as she died first."

"Her parents were supposed to be buried with her, but they found that the ground where she was buried was very rocky." Henri shook his head. "Emilie's was a single burial in that plot. And they only found that out the day of her burial."

"How sad," Norma said. "I noticed there was usually two or more people interred in each grave there."

"There was talk about moving her to be with her parents," Henri said, "but no one had the money back then, and everyone just wanted them to rest in peace." He pulled a leather folder from his satchel and laid out a half-finished genealogy chart across the table. Names, dates, and tiny notes sprawled in neat rows, but there were gaps like missing teeth where branches had yet to be filled.

Graham studied it. "I need to make one for the Brody clan."

"This," Henri said at last, tapping the paper, "will be as complete as I can make it before the school year is out. And when it is, I will bring a copy back here, to place beside your own records. Our families deserve to see how the branches intertwine."

Graham looked at him steadily. "And when that time comes, I'll go south with you to Montreal," he said. "I'd like to meet your family."

Henri's expression softened into something close to gratitude. "They would welcome you. My uncle René will insist on pouring you too much wine, and my cousin Elise will ask a hundred questions about life in New Brunswick."

"I'll have to get to work on my Brody side now, especially my grandfather," Graham said. "I'd like to fill up your chart with as much as I can find. And I can't argue that I'm even more interested in my ancestors than I was before."

Henri rose. "I'd like that. But now, I've taken enough of your time for now." He extended his hand. Graham clasped it firmly.

"You'll keep in touch?" Graham asked.

"Of course. And you, mon cousin, must keep a chair ready by this fire. When I return, I will have a story to tell, and perhaps a family to introduce."

Graham stood on the porch and watched Henri's car pull away gently, kicking up only a little dust. He was sorry his father would never know of these relatives, but he looked forward to meeting this branch of the tree, soon.

Chapter Twenty-Three

The sky above Paris was feathered with clouds as Ellie and Quinn made their way through the terminal, dragging rolling suitcases behind them. The long glass walls reflected their slightly rumpled figures, and beyond, the runways glowed with the blinking red and white lights of aircraft preparing for departure. Ellie carried herself with the quiet energy of someone who had slept her last night of her honeymoon in broken fragments, her hair twisted up haphazardly, but her eyes bright with the anticipation of returning home. Quinn, more deliberate in his movements, kept his passport tucked carefully into his jacket pocket, one hand always brushing the zipper of his carry-on as if checking it was still there.

"Gate E28," Ellie said, glancing at the overhead monitor. "That's us."

Quinn nodded, adjusting the strap of his bag. "I'll be happy once we're actually on the plane. Security always feels like the longest part."

Ellie laughed softly. "I thought you handled it like a pro. You didn't even blink when they pulled your bag aside."

"That's because I knew it was just the charger cord," he replied with a grin. "Not some international incident."

They walked side by side down the terminal, past boutiques and cafés where sleepy travelers nursed espressos in paper cups. Ellie inhaled deeply, catching one last note of croissant and roasted coffee drifting from a bakery kiosk. "This is the part I'll miss the most," she admitted.

Quinn gave her hand a quick squeeze. "Don't let Maggie hear you say Paris pastries are better than hers. And we'll be back someday. Right now, I just want to be home."

At the gate, the line was already forming. Families clustered with strollers, business travelers tapped on phones, and a few exhausted students slumped in seats. The announcements switched between French and English, the clipped tones familiar and soothing. Ellie and Quinn scanned their boarding passes, exchanged polite bonjours with the staff, and walked down the jet bridge into the plane.

Ellie settled into her window seat, pressing her forehead briefly against the cool glass before buckling in. Paris glittered beneath them once the plane rose, the city shrinking to a scatter of lights, the Eiffel Tower gleaming faintly in the distance before vanishing into cloud.

"I'm surprised you chose the window seat," Quinn murmured beside her.

Ellie turned away from the view. "I just wanted to see the last of Paris. Doesn't mean I'll be staring at the clouds."

The long hours of the flight blurred into a rhythm of films on the seatback screens, occasional conversations, and the muted clink of cutlery when the attendants rolled carts down the aisles. They chose the simple chicken dinner option.

Ellie picked at the potatoes first. "Do you think Cali knows what day it is?" she asked suddenly, smiling at the thought.

Quinn swallowed a piece of bread. "You mean that we're coming home today? Dogs always know. She probably sat at the door all morning, waiting."

"I'm sure she's doing fine, but... you know how she gets. She's going to be beside herself."

Quinn chuckled. "So will we. Honestly, the best part of traveling is that moment when you open your own door again."

Ellie leaned back, imagining the farmhouse: the wide porch, the tall maples that lined the drive, and Cali bounding down the steps toward them. Her heart gave a small tug.

Hours later, when the captain announced their descent into Montreal, Ellie felt the hum of excitement rise again. Below them, the St. Lawrence River gleamed in the late afternoon sun, winding between clusters of buildings. The plane dipped smoothly, the familiar sprawl of the city drawing closer.

It was just past 5:30 when they stepped off the plane and into the cool, conditioned air of Montréal–Trudeau International Airport. The terminal was bright and bustling, filled with the overlapping sound of French and English conversations, announcements echoing from overhead speakers, and the wheeled percussion of countless suitcases. It was as if they'd never left France.

They moved quickly through customs, the officer barely glancing up after stamping their passports. Quinn exhaled with relief. "That was painless."

Ellie nodded, her thoughts already moving ahead to the next steps. They collected their bags, found the shuttle to the long-term parking lot, and soon were reunited with their car. The vehicle looked slightly dusty from its week of sitting, but otherwise unchanged, a comforting sight after so many days in unfamiliar places.

Quinn popped the trunk, heaved their suitcases in, and slid behind the wheel. Ellie buckled into the passenger seat, already yawning. "If we time it right," she murmured, "we'll be pulling into Percyville by seven-thirty."

"That's the goal," Quinn replied, turning the key. The car purred to life, the radio coming on faintly with a local sports station talking about the Montreal Canadiens' prospects for the new hockey season. As they pulled out of the lot, the sinking sun painted the sky in pale streaks of gold and rose.

The road stretched ahead, familiar yet fresh to eyes having spent days scanning foreign landscapes. Traffic thickened briefly around the airport, then thinned as they turned onto the quieter highways leading them home. Ellie dozed off, her head against the window, the rhythm of the tires lulling her. Quinn glanced at her, turned down the radio, and drove in steady silence.

By the time Ellie stirred awake, the fields outside were deepening into shadow. She stretched and looked around, instantly recognizing landmarks: a red barn set close to the road, the wide dip where the river curved, the hand-painted sign for an orchard that sold cider in autumn. "We're close," she said softly, her voice warm with anticipation.

Quinn smiled without taking his eyes off the road. "Almost there."

They turned down the gravel drive at last, the tires crunching familiarly beneath them. The farmhouse came into view, its porch light glowing warmly against the dusk. Ellie's heart leapt at the sight. Even from the car, she could see movement on the porch: Shirley, Ruth, and Jeremy, gathered with easy smiles as if waiting for this very moment.

Cali was there too. At the sound of the car, she bounded down the steps, tail wagging so furiously her whole body shook with it. Ellie barely had the car door open before Cali was upon her, pressing a wet nose into her hands, whining with joy.

"Cali!" Ellie laughed, dropping to her knees on the gravel. The dog's paws pressed against her shoulders, tongue lapping at her cheek. Ellie wrapped her arms around the warm, wriggling body. "I missed you so much."

Quinn joined in, ruffling Cali's fur. "You've been taking good care of the place, haven't you, girl?"

From the porch, Shirley called, "Welcome home, travelers!" Her voice carried across the yard, full of cheer.

Ruth and Jeremy waved, and Ellie felt a surge of gratitude. "We made it," she called back, still kneeling with Cali.

Shirley ushered them inside, and the interior smelled like home the moment they stepped across the threshold: a blend of wood, faint lilac from the sachets Ruth liked to leave in drawers, and, Ellie realized suddenly, freshly baked goods. On the kitchen table sat a neat arrangement of wrapped parcels: loaves of bread, a plate of cookies, and a pie cooling on a rack.

"You didn't have to..." Ellie began, touched.

Shirley waved her off. "Nonsense. We wanted you to come home to something cozy. And Maggie was more than willing to supply them."

Jeremy added, "Everything's tidy, fridge is stocked with basics, and Cali's been walked every day. Having Samantha drop by as much as she did has been a blessing. She ran and played with Cali until she needed as many naps as we did."

Cali barked once as if in agreement, then pressed herself against Ellie's leg again.

Quinn set the suitcases by the stairs. "You three are lifesavers."

"We're just glad you're back safe," Ruth said warmly. "Traveling's exciting, but nothing beats coming home."

They lingered for a while, catching up on small details: the weather that had shifted from summer's heat toward autumn's coolness, a neighbor who had stopped by to drop off mail accidently delivered to them, the raccoon making a brief nuisance of itself near the compost but had since disappeared.

At last Shirley gathered her bag. "We'll leave you two to settle in. But there's dinner in the oven; Tourtière. Just needs reheating if you're hungry later."

Ellie's eyes shone. "You really thought of everything."

"Oh," Shirley stopped, a mischievous glint in her eye. "We're having a meeting tomorrow, ten o'clock at the Café. Graham has some news to share. He, Norma and Phil went on a road trip while you were gone."

"What?" Ellie asked, eyes open wide.

Ruth patted her arm. "We know nothing of the details, just that it's exciting."

"Then I'll definitely be there," Ellie assured them.

"As will I," Quinn added.

"And you'll tell us all about your discoveries as well," Shirley said, pointing her finger at Ellie. "We know you found something because you're left eye is twitching. It's a dead giveaway. But now's the time to relax."

The friends exchanged hugs at the door, promised to be prompt for the morning's meeting, and then the car headlights swept down the drive, leaving the farmhouse quiet once more.

Ellie grabbed a toy off the porch and watched Cali dash off and head towards the path into the woods. "I guess you don't need asking twice."

Quinn pulled on a jacket, and together they stepped out into the cool evening air. The sky was dusky violet now, the first stars pricking through. Fallen leaves crunched beneath their shoes as they entered the woods, Cali trotting eagerly ahead, before turning and waiting for her toy to fly through the air.

The walk carried them past the treehouse, across the wooden bridge, past the pond, and through the apple orchard; the soft chirp of crickets rising all around. The world felt hushed, a counterpoint to the constant bustle of Paris. Ellie breathed deeply, filling her lungs with the earthy, familiar air.

"Doesn't it feel like everything slowed down here while we were gone?" she asked softly.

Quinn nodded. "I can't believe how much I've missed the calm."

They walked in companionable silence for a while, Cali darting off into the deep woods when Quinn flung the toy. Occasionally she looked back, ears perked, making sure they were still with her. Each time she came close to drop the toy at Quinn's feet, Ellie reached down to ruffle her fur, her heart warming at the dog's joy.

By the time they returned to the farmhouse, the porch light glowed brighter against the darkness. The house seemed to embrace them with its stillness. Inside, the tourtière waited.

Ellie leaned against the doorframe for a moment, letting the simple scene settle over her. "Home," she whispered.

Quinn slipped an arm around her shoulders. "Home," he echoed, before picking her up, to her delighted squeals, and carried her across the threshold.

Cali gave a small bark, as if sealing the word with her own approval, and wagged her tail until the whole room seemed to glow with her happiness.

Chapter Twenty-Four

The autumn air had a crisp edge to it, turning cheeks pink and making the steam of hot drinks feel like a blessing. Maggie's Cozy Corner Café, with its weathered cedar shingles and wide windows looking out on the maple-lined road, seemed to glow like a lantern in the early morning light. Inside, the warm scent of cinnamon and butter floated through the air, mingling with the faint clink of teacups and the gentle murmur of conversation. The café was quiet at this hour, between the opening crowd and before lunch crowd, which made it the perfect place for the Heritage Harvesters to gather.

Maggie herself bustled from the kitchen, her apron dusted with flour, balancing a tray piled high with oatmeal raisin cookies, molasses crinkles, and a teapot with enough amber liquid to keep them all talking for hours. She set the tray on the round table in the back room, where the sun slanted in at just the right angle to make the polished wood glow.

"Here we are," she said, brushing her hands on her apron and smiling at the group that was gradually settling into their chairs. "Fresh from the oven. Don't make me bring any of it back, either."

Ruth was the first to reach for a cookie, her laugh bright and teasing. "You never have to worry about that, Maggie. We'll see to it." She nudged Jeremy, who was already pouring the tea with steady, careful hands.

"Save me one of those molasses ones," Shirley called as she hung her jacket over the back of her chair. Ruth's sister had a knack for entering a room with a kind of breezy assurance, as if she'd been there all along.

If you didn't know her, you'd say Shirley was a tad aggressive, until you realized she had one of the biggest hearts around. She reached across to give Maggie's arm a squeeze. "Smells divine, sweetheart. You'll spoil us."

"I plan to," Maggie replied, pulling out a chair. Graham had asked her specifically to join this meeting, as the information he had to share included her.

At the far end of the table, Aunt Norma plopped into her seat, not taking off her sweater just yet. Phil took the chair beside her, his presence quiet but reassuring. Both wore the faintly tired expressions of travelers who had lately been places worth talking about.

Graham hovered for a moment, almost restless, before taking the seat across from Maggie. He was trying not to look too eager, but his eyes betrayed him; they sparkled with the light of someone carrying a story too good to keep. Maggie knew he had found something exciting on his trip with Norma and Phil, but was patient enough to wait. Barely.

Ellie and Quinn arrived last, the newlyweds, their hands linked as if the world hadn't yet managed to pry them apart. Ellie carried a small wrapped parcel, which she held with care. Quinn held their larger bag of gifts. They slipped into the remaining chairs, their faces still carrying the sunlit glow of honeymoon days.

The group was complete, except for Tess, who had promised to make the next meeting. The Heritage Harvesters, all gathered in Maggie's café, all bringing pieces of their journeys to the table.

It didn't take long before the conversation quieted, attention turning naturally toward Graham. He shifted in his chair, cleared his throat, and looked down at his folded hands. Then, as if unable to contain himself, he leaned forward. "I wanted to share this with you all together," he said, his voice low but brimming with excitement. "Norma, Phil, and I had the most remarkable trip to Baie-Saint-Paul. And, well, I found something. A connection. A *real* one."

The table stilled. Maggie's hand froze halfway to the teapot, her eyes widening.

"You mean...?" Ruth prompted gently.

"Yes," Graham said. His voice wavered on the word, but he pressed on, eager now. "I mean family. I found Lucien. But I never expected..." He paused, took a deep breath. "While we were in Baie-Saint-Paul, we visited the old farmhouse and found a branch of my tree."

Norma leaned forward, her eyes gleaming. "Tell them about Henri," she urged.

Graham's answering smile erased years from his features. "When we got back from our trip, my DNA results were waiting. With Norma's help," he cast her a warm smile and she shrugged her shoulders as if it was nothing, "...I was able to find a close match to Lucien's family."

"We met him," Norma said.

Graham nodded, his fingers tapping on the table. "Yesterday afternoon he came by to visit."

"He's a very nice young man," Norma added.

"He's Lucien's grandson, through his second marriage. He's doing a final project in his sociology masters degree about family genealogy. He was thrilled to meet me and shared a lot about the family, filling in blanks I didn't know. Can you imagine? He sat in my living room and spoke of ancestors as if they'd just stepped out for a walk. He knew a lot of the names, but he also had details I never dreamed we'd find about the living relatives. He made the past feel alive."

There was a collective intake of breath around the table. Jeremy leaned back, his smile spreading slowly, while Shirley clapped her hands together once, sharp and delighted.

Ellie sat stunned. "I can't believe all this happened while we were away."

"And it doesn't end there," Graham went on, his voice shaking with the sheer joy of it. "Henri told me there are more, many more, living in Montreal. Cousins, distant and close, some who've kept the old stories alive. I'm going to meet them soon. Can you imagine? From finding an envelope of letters one day to having a whole branch of family I never knew existed a week later."

For a moment, no one spoke. The weight of it, the miracle of connection across time and distance, hung in the air like incense.

Maggie was the first to break the silence. Her eyes were shining, though she tried to blink away the tears. "Grandad," she whispered. "This is amazing. I'm so happy for you."

"I wanted to tell you what we found when we're all together," Graham said, his voice gentling as he looked at her. "This isn't just for me. It's for all of us. Our roots, our story. And to be with you now, Maggie... knowing you'll carry it forward..." His words faltered, and he reached across the table, taking her hand. "It means everything."

Maggie squeezed back, her smile trembling but radiant. "Then we'll carry it together."

After the flurry of congratulations and cookies being passed around, Ellie set the small package she'd been carrying on the table. Her expression was thoughtful, touched with that new-married glow but also with a seriousness that drew everyone's attention.

"Quinn and I have a story too," she said softly. "Something we discovered on our honeymoon. Quinn surprised me by arranging to spend a couple of days in the town my Ethier ancestors are from. We got to walk where they walked. And we found something I didn't expect."

Quinn nodded, urging her on, his thumb brushing against her knuckles in encouragement.

Ellie took a breath. "I finally learned why my ancestor came to Quebec hundreds of years ago. All I ever knew was the date he arrived. But I never understood the reason. And now I do." Her voice wavered, steadied. "His wife and child died in a fire. That was what drove him to leave everything behind. He crossed the ocean for a new life. It was during the time of French settlers being needed in Quebec and he took advantage of that. He had a trade as a shoemaker, and that was an important aspect of him being able to move. They needed him here. And he needed a new beginning, perhaps even a refuge from his loss."

Around the table, heads bowed slightly, as if in respect for a grief centuries old but still resonant.

Ellie continued, her voice hushed but clear. "Learning that changed the way I see him. It changed the way I see myself, too. His survival, his choice to keep living; it's part of why we're here today. Out of that sorrow came a legacy that reached all the way to me."

Her eyes shimmered with tears, but she smiled. "And on the same journey, we met someone important. Aunt Norma, this is for you." She pushed the parcel gently across the table.

Norma blinked in surprise, then slowly unwrapped the paper. Inside was a carefully wrapped box, and inside the box was a USB stick, tied with ribbon. She looked up at Ellie, confused but hopeful.

"From Claudette," Ellie said softly. "I gave her your gift, and when we saw her on our last day, she asked that I give this to you."

For a moment, Norma could only stare, her eyes filling. And then she laughed. "Claudette..." she whispered, the name a prayer on her lips. "Never a woman to be one-upped. I think I know what this is. It's history—our history. Gosh, *my* history."

Phil laid a gentle hand on her arm, steadying her as the tears came freely. Around the table, there was no rush to fill the silence. They let it stretch, sacred and tender, until Norma dabbed her eyes with a handkerchief and smiled through the tears.

"Thank you," she said, her voice thick but sure. "Thank you for bringing this to me."

"And we bought everyone a little something from across the ocean," Quinn added, passing around the gifts they had chosen for their friends. Everyone was delighted and hugs given.

From there, the conversation flowed as easily as the tea. They passed the last of the cookies and stories in equal measure, laughter bubbling up between moments of quiet reverence. Each person added something; memories, questions, small reflections, knitting the group tighter still.

Phil spoke of how the journey had changed his sense of belonging. Shirley joked about trying some of the recipes from their mother's cookbook they had just found. Ruth and Jeremy groaned. Shirley was not a good cook.

Maggie, still a little overwhelmed, kept listening, absorbing. She realized she was part of something larger than she had ever imagined; not just the café she ran, or the community she loved, but a web of family stretching across oceans and centuries.

The café itself seemed to hold them, the golden light deepening as the sun rose higher, the world outside buzzing with life. It was, unmistakably, a final chapter; but not an ending. More like the moment when you close one book, knowing another waits on the shelf.

And when at last the teapot was empty and the cookie plate reduced to crumbs, Graham leaned back with a satisfied sigh. "Look at us," he said, his voice filled with quiet wonder. "Each of us carrying a piece of the story. Each of us adding to it. If that isn't a harvest, I don't know what is."

Ruth gazed at her friends and smiled. "In the smallest of houses, under the quietest roofs, the loudest legacies live."

"I want that on a t-shirt," Norma said, making them all laugh.

They raised their cups in a makeshift toast; tea, not wine, but no less sacred.

"To the harvest," Ruth said, her voice strong.

"To the family," added Ellie.

"To the stories," Quinn said.

And together, voices mingling, they answered: "To us."

THE END

Thank You!

To my Readers,

Thank you for taking the time to read Family Past. The kind words I've received for the whole series is greatly appreciated.

Please note that all books are available in large print, and you can find all ebooks in the series at your local library. If they don't have them, ask. Librarians are amazing!

If you'd like to help other readers find new authors, please consider leaving a review and sharing my books with friends. Your support means the world to me.

You can leave a review on my website, Amazon, or Goodreads.

If you'd like to receive my newsletter, you'll receive a **free PDF of over 100 Oral History Questions** to help you start writing your own personal history (*or memoir as Shirley likes to refer to it*). You'll also get advance notice of my new books and recommendations of books that I'm currently reading, and first look at the blog topic of the month. Hope to see you there!

And I'd love to hear from you! Drop me a line at beth@bethfarrar.com and share what you've been up to in your own family research. Being a family detective is exciting!

Thank you again for all your support,

Beth

About the author

Beth Farrar has been writing stories since her parents handed her a library card. Oftentimes reading five books at a time, her imagination was sparked. Encouragement from English teachers then set her on a serious path of learning the craft throughout her life.

From writing TV scripts to full length movies for pleasure and practice, she developed her writing skills by exploring various mediums. Filling notebooks with ideas, sketching characters and locations, and inventing sticky situations for characters to survive, is Beth's happy place (besides walking through cemeteries, but that's another story!).

For fifteen years Beth wrote a monthly column, Living Country, in her local English language newspaper, Main Street, sharing interesting observations about living and raising her three sons in the country with her husband. Having always loved genealogy, Beth melded two of her passions together and created the Ellie McLellan Genealogy Mystery series.

For tips and tricks on how to write your own personal history story, visit Beth's website bethfarrar.com and join her newsletter to get a free Oral History Questions booklet to start your journey writing your own personal story. You'll find interesting blog posts, and be first to learn when new books are on the way!

Acknowledgements

A writer creates a story, but so many other people help bring it to light.

First of all, without **you amazing readers**, I'd just be writing for myself! Which I used to do, but now it's more fun to share and talk about characters that we wish were real!

Ronnie Pelletier, my splendiferous editor. It's funny how a writer can be so in the flow that they forget which tense they're writing in. But you never let me forget, and for that, I'm immensely grateful!

Teresa O'Neil, my number one reader, who keeps me on target and without fail points out things I should have seen (without her doing this, well, I shudder to think). Your input is invaluable.

Daphne Petersen, my eagle eyed proofreader and suggestion maker. You taught my sons how to write properly, and I'm thankful that you can still teach this old dog new tricks (or when to use semi-colons!!!).

My family, you guys encourage me every day and you'll never understand how much that means to me. Merci!

Afterword

Would you like to write your own personal story? Join my newsletter at bethfarrar.com where you'll find a free PDF with 100+ questions that you can use to start your journey. You'll also find more topics in my blog about how to start assembling your own life story.

Ellie helped a few people solve genealogy mysteries in this book using methods that you can apply as well:

1. **Who is the oldest ancestor you know of?** Do you have a picture of them, any documents giving information? Gather what you can and place the ancestor in the history of the day. Look in history books or online newspapers and find out what life was like for them. What was their occupation? How has it changed over the years? What traits do you share?

2. **Have you had any interesting DNA matches in your research?** What surprises have you found, and have you reached out to any new relative? Was it a good outcome? And if you haven't reached out, why not?

3. **Locate a town or city where a distant ancestor came from or lived**. If you can, go visit it and walk in their footsteps. Find the homes they lived or worked in, and learn about the place's history. Locate historical photos of the place and recent ones to compare. Does the home they lived in still exist?

Printed in Dunstable, United Kingdom

74715859R00117